A HERO'S KISS

"Are you all right, Rachel?" Colin came to her and put his hands on her shoulders, pulling her gauzy cap sleeves back into place.

"I am. He frightened me, but in retrospect, I can see he thought I would welcome his kisses. I just had been daydreaming and had not realized how far we had strayed." She could not exactly tell Colin she had been daydreaming about him.

His expression serious, Colin said, "You must be careful, Rach. You are so beautiful. More than one man could be tempted to hope you would favor him."

"My beauty does not excuse his behavior," she said, stung by the implication that she was somehow responsible for Featherfew's misbehavior.

"Of course not. I did not mean that. But you are so lovely . . ." He let the sentence hang, and there was silence between them.

Then the extraordinary happened.

His expression softened and his dark eyes blazed like coal. He surrounded Rachel with his arms and pulled her close, hesitated for just a moment, and then kissed her. . . .

Books by Donna Simpson

LORD ST. CLAIRE'S ANGEL

LADY DELAFONT'S DILEMMA

LADY MAY'S FOLLY

MISS TRUELOVE BECKONS

BELLE OF THE BALL

A RAKE'S REDEMPTION

A COUNTRY COURTSHIP

A MATCHMAKER'S CHRISTMAS

PAMELA'S SECOND SEASON

RACHEL'S CHANGE OF HEART

Published by Zebra Books

RACHEL'S CHANGE OF HEART

Donna Simpson

ZEBRA BOOKS
Kensington Publishing Corp.
http://www.kensingtonbooks.com

One

Rachel gazed steadily at her younger sister, Pamela, gloriously spring-like in her moss green wedding gown. Pamela sat at one end of the long table in the Haven House dining room, with her new husband, Lord Strongwycke, at her side. Something was wrong with the picture. It was . . . misty. Rachel touched her eyes with one gloved hand and felt moisture seep through the fine silk of her gloves.

She was crying. She swallowed hard around a knotted lump in her throat and looked to the left and then to the right at her elegant fiancé, Lord Yarnell, and her grandmother, hoping no one had seen her mystifying descent into maudlin sentiment. It would not do to have anyone think her less than composed and ladylike.

But . . . Pamela was so utterly lovely, a vision in pale green silk with a circlet of ivory roses on her auburn curls and a glowing necklace of perfectly matched pearls around her slender neck. Rachel, mortified, felt the tears begin to trickle down her cheeks and drip unheeded from her chin. Her nose started to run, and she tried to sniffle without anyone noticing. *What is wrong with me?* she thought. *Surely I do not envy my sister her husband.*

Someone was making a ribald toast. Heaven preserve them all, it was Grandmother, and the old lady was being crude again! No matter that the snowy-tressed *grande dame* was dressed elegantly in azure satin and diamonds, she still allowed her earthy wit free rein.

It wouldn't do even to think about what Grandmother was saying, but it had to do with the marital bed and—Rachel clutched her hands together under the lace-covered table and glanced once again at her fiancé, hoping he would not take offense. Yarnell was so very proper and stiff, formal in his manners. It was one of the things she had found to admire in him. He would never make a scene or embarrass one with emotional outbursts.

Not like—

She glanced across the table at Sir Colin Varens, a family friend and neighbor of the viscount Lord Haven—Rachel's older brother—and his family, north in Yorkshire. They had all known each other forever, but of late Rachel had been avoiding the baronet and his weird sister, especially since they had descended unexpectedly upon London in all their bucolic unsuitableness. At least now that she was engaged to be married he would not propose to her again, and that was some comfort.

Colin cleared his throat noisily. "I, too, propose a toast," he said, standing. He smiled down the long table at the newlyweds, his homely face registering all the joy of the occasion. "Here is to long life, long love, and hope for the future."

"Hear, hear," his sister said, her voice revealing her tipsy state as she raised her glass.

"And here is to intelligent choices," Grand said. "And good-looking, strong husbands and warm beds."

Pamela threw back her head and laughed, then gasped as her new husband did something naughty behind her back. There was general laughter, which even Belinda, Strongwycke's young niece, joined in, although she looked a little bewildered. Rachel pinched her lips together and wondered when her family and friends would ever stop embarrassing her. She could see a similar look of disapproval on her mother's face, across the table from her.

"Kiss the bride, Strongwycke," Colin hollered, winking across the table at the dowager.

"Yes, kiss her! Give her something to think about!" Grandmother hammered on the table with her knobby, arthritic fist.

The sun streamed in through a gap in the curtain and touched the couple standing at the end of the table. Strongwycke gazed down at his slight bride and silence fell over the company. There was no mistaking the look on his handsome countenance. Tenderness, affection, joy—all were equally displayed, along with something else, something warmer and more intimate. As he took Pamela in his arms and pulled her close, kissing her mouth, Rachel felt again the pang of envy. They were so in love. She looked at her little sister's beaming countenance when the new groom was done. No one could mistake that look for anything but the glow of love. She glanced once more at her groom-to-be, Lord Yarnell, and saw the rigid expression of distaste on his face.

"This will all be over in a few minutes," Rachel whispered, putting her hand over his on the table.

He withdrew his gloved hand quickly. "I should hope so. I am not used to displays of this kind in public."

"They're not always like this," Rachel pleaded. "My family can be as circumspect as anyone, but this *is* a special occasion."

Yarnell harrumphed and fell silent.

The meal and multitude of toasts following it were over at last, and everyone accompanied the bride and groom out the front door to their waiting carriage. They were going north, first to stop off and visit Pamela and Rachel's newlywed brother, Lord Haven, and his bride, Jane, at Haven Court in Yorkshire—because of the suddenness of the marriage, the viscount and his new wife had not had time to travel south for the ceremony—and then they were going on to Strongwycke's home, Shadow Manor, in the Lakes District. At her special request, they were leaving behind his niece, Belinda, the headstrong girl who had been the catalyst of their meeting, to stay in London with Sir Colin Varens and his odd, but endearing to some people, sister, Andromeda. The girl, just thirteen, had become fast friends with Andromeda, and was to stay with her new ally for a month while Strongwycke and Pamela had some time alone together.

The gathered company all crowded through the narrow doorway into the late spring sunshine of the London street in front of Haven House—a tall, narrow, ugly London town home—descended the steps, and stood on the walk outside as Pamela and Strongwycke climbed into his elegant traveling equipage.

Pamela's mother said a tearful farewell to her least favorite child. Then Sir Colin and Andromeda said good-bye, shaking hands with both the bride and groom through the open window of the carriage. Belinda clung to her new aunt's hands for the longest time, and unexpectedly burst into tears, then ran back into the house, followed by a concerned Andromeda. Sir Colin reassured the couple that the child would be just fine and followed his sister into the house.

Pamela beckoned to Rachel, who reluctantly approached the carriage. She was glad Yarnell had opted to wait inside while everyone else said their good-byes to the new couple. It would never do for him to see his fiancée tear up as she had at the dinner table.

"Look after her, Rach," Pamela said, leaning out the window and casting a worried glance up at the house. A carriage trundled by past Strongwycke's carriage and the team shied.

"Look after Belinda? I understood she was staying with Andromeda and Colin."

"She is, but I would just feel better if you would look in on her every once in a while and write to me."

Rachel felt a budding of warmth for her highly emotional little sister, and took her bare hand. It was so small, she reflected, looking down at it and the lovely pearl and diamond ring on her wedding finger. And yet Pamela had become a woman in their short London Season, finding a

husband that any lady would envy in the Earl of
Strongwycke. "I will do it for you, Pammy,"
Rachel said, lifting the small hand and rubbing
her own cheek with it. "Now go," she said, releasing her sister's hand. "Go and don't worry
about anything. Go and be happy!" The treach-
erous tears threatened again and Rachel blinked
them back.

"I will," Pamela said, her voice trembling. She
glanced over her shoulder at her handsome
groom, waiting patiently and smiling at the two
sisters. "I know I'll be happy. I love him so much,"
she whispered. She gazed back into her older sister's eyes, and the green became misty with
worry. "Oh, Rach, do anything rather than marry
without love!" she exclaimed.

Strongwycke murmured something to Pamela
as he touched her shoulder, and she nodded, saying, "I know we have to go. I am ready." She
reached out of the carriage one more time and
squeezed her sister's hand. "I mean it, Rach. Do
anything rather than marry without love."

Rachel remained silent, knowing her voice
would be clogged with tears and unwilling to display her emotion so openly. The earl called to
the driver, and the handsome team of grays
started on the journey. Rachel stood alone on the
pavement for a long few minutes, watching the
carriage trundle down the street toward the road
out of London, the road north to their home.
Brilliant sun gleamed off the lanterns, and a
fresh breeze riffled the plumed headdress on the
horses. Then they turned the corner and were
gone.

Gone. Gone together to their new life. No little sister anymore, but a married woman, and likely, soon enough, mother of a cheery brood, judging by the glint in the earl's eye. Just like that the child became a woman. It seemed only moments had passed since Pamela was racing across the moors and up and down the fells of Yorkshire in joyous abandon, but those days were gone forever.

Rachel finally turned and stared up at the tall, dark house, one of a line of several tall, dark, narrow houses joined together and sharing walls. The façades, once clean stone, were now dark with coal smoke. She thought about her sister's last words. Pamela just did not understand. Some people were made for love, and some people inspired it. Everyone loved Pamela. How could one not? She was funny and sweet and impetuous, good-natured, endearingly naive.

All the things Rachel was not. *I am cold like ice and hard like diamonds,* she thought, trying to derive comfort from that thought. She made her way up the steps into the front hall past the butler, who held the door open for her, then closed it firmly and retreated to his other duties. Rachel stood in the gloomy hallway listening to the babble of cheerful noise as everyone, from the sounds of it, competed to make Belinda forget the touching scene they had just taken part in. Soon the girl's voice was raised in laughter.

Rachel did not want to join them, even though her fiancé, the eminently suitable marquess Lord Yarnell, was there, probably mortally offended by half the cheery games now taking place. Sighing deeply, she knew she could not just retreat upstairs, which was all she really wanted to do. She wanted to crawl into her bed and pull the covers over her head. Why was she feeling so low? This should signal the beginning of her true enjoyment of the Season. She was engaged and could relax now. She had found her ideal life partner, an irreproachable man of distinction.

Now was her hour of triumph; she would plan, with her mother, a spectacular wedding to celebrate that triumph, then settle into the life she was born to lead.

The doors to the drawing room opened and Colin slipped out into the dim hallway. "I thought I would find you here. I don't know why, I just did." He moved toward her in the gloom, his dark eyes shadowed by his thick eyebrows.

Rachel stepped back into the shadows of the staircase, loath to let her old friend and erstwhile suitor see the tears standing in her eyes. "I . . . was just coming to join everyone. Is Belinda all right?"

"She's fine. She just was overcome with the emotion of the moment, I think. But Andromeda has her laughing now over some conundrum she has written. Andy is a great one for puzzles, you know." He moved, still, toward her.

Rachel melted back farther into the shadows. "She always was. When we were children, she could keep us amused for hours with riddles and picture puzzles. I had forgotten about that until now."

Colin took a deep breath and reached out, wanting to take Rachel by the shoulders. She shrank away, evading his grasp, and he could not but interpret her movement as distaste for even his touch. He had brought it on himself, he supposed, by his repeated unwelcome attentions over the years. That was all over now. She was an engaged woman, and he was over the silly infatuation that had made him her slave for so many years. But now he must show her that she need not avoid him. He would be a man about this.

"Rachel," he said, keeping his voice calm and even as he let his arms fall back to his sides, "have no fear. All I want from you now is your friendship."

She was silent. Her pale face glowed in the shadows, lighting up even the gloom of the dim hallway with her loveliness. Her eyes, the blue of the Yorkshire sky after a cleansing rain, gleamed softly in the thin thread of light from the parlor.

He took a deep, steadying breath and moved forward again. Taking her in his arms, he hugged her tightly, consciously ignoring the curvaceousness of her form. "Believe me, my old friend, I understand now how unwelcome my attentions were all those years and I most sincerely apologize for making you uneasy. All I want now is for us to be comfortable together."

She laid her head on his shoulder and sighed deeply, all the tension draining from her sweet frame.

He felt a rush of warmth. "That's good," he said, though she had not answered him in words. "That's good." He patted her head, feeling the soft curls wind around his blunt fingers.

But he pushed her away finally, and said, cheerily, "There, now we can be friendly. I am so glad my absurd infatuation is over and I can see clearly now that we would not have suited. In fact, two less suitable people in the world could not be, am I right?" He forced a jocularity into his tone that he did not quite feel.

"Right," she said, her tone brittle. She stood straight and said, "Let us rejoin the company, then. I have a wedding to plan, you know."

Colin threw a glance at the closed door of the drawing room. "You do mean to marry him, then?"

"Of course! I am engaged, Colin. I thought we had established that." She gazed at him, her eyebrows drawn together.

"It is just that he is . . ." He broke off, feeling the heat rise in his cheeks. "I will say no more. Just because the fellow does not suit my tastes doesn't mean a thing, I suppose. Andy is always telling me I have no idea of elegance, nor any pretensions to refinement."

"Andromeda is right," Rachel said, dryly.

Colin chuckled. "Good, you can abuse me as a friend. I like that." He took her arm and guided her back toward the drawing room. "Let us rejoin the company."

The day ended with an early dinner, and then the company broke up, Andromeda and Colin retreating with Belinda to Lord Strongwycke's town house. The earl had asked if the brother and sister would like to stay there for the remainder of the Season with his niece, since they were doing him the favor of caring for her. They would then travel north with the girl and take her to Shadow Manor before heading to Corleigh, their own home in Yorkshire, near Haven Court.

Shortly after everyone retreated, Lord Yarnell was about to take his leave. Rachel's mother, in recognition of their new status as an engaged couple, gave them a half hour alone together in the drawing room.

Rachel sat demurely, her hands folded together, on the dingy sofa, one of the many pieces that her mother had not had time to replace before Pamela's nuptial breakfast. She waited for Yarnell to speak, hoping he would say something warm, something out of character. She did not understand herself at that moment, since his elegant coolness had drawn her initially to him. She had felt from the beginning that they were alike, and suited to each other. And yet she was haunted by the warmth of the look Strongwycke had given Pamela before shockingly kissing her so publicly at the wedding breakfast. It had been so full of yearning. Affection. Devotion.

Desire.

Shocking thought. She turned away from it. She gazed up at her fiancé as he paced on the new carpet in front of her. "What did you think of my sister's wedding, my lord?"

"I do not think I have ever seen a less elegant wedding coat than Lord Strongwycke's." He sat beside her and crossed his legs. "And I thought your grandmother's toast very coarse."

"It is just her way," Rachel said, not sure why she was defending her family when she had been thinking the same things. "She is from a different time, and has a different sense of humor."

"Sir Colin's was just as distasteful."

Rachel frowned and thought that all Colin had done was toast long life and happiness in the future. What was wrong with that? But she kept her thoughts to herself.

Yarnell, his gloves finally discarded, polished his nails on his breeches and stared down at them. "I have been thinking of our wedding breakfast. Do you think, if my mother holds it at our town house, that your grandmother may find it too fatiguing to go?"

She and her grandmother had never had the closest of relationships, but Rachel was stung that he was obliquely trying to find a way to exclude her. "She has great stamina when she wants to do something, and I cannot imagine she would not want to come."

"But you do not like her. You have said so."

"No, I said we did not always agree. I would never say something so disloyal as that I did not like her. She is my grandmother, Yarnell, and she will want to be at my wedding breakfast. She will not be able to make it into the church, I do not think, given the steps, but surely she is welcome at my wedding breakfast!"

"I did not say she would be unwelcome. She may well embarrass you, though, my dear. I flatter myself that we think alike on most subjects, and I found her remarks coarse and lewd."

Rachel clamped her lips together. She felt like she was suffocating and wanted nothing more than for Yarnell to leave so she could strip off her gloves—he did not approve of ladies having ungloved hands, he had told her once, and so she had kept them on much longer than necessary—and shed her stays and go to bed. She longed to crawl into her bed, pull the covers over her head and cry. It would feel so very good at that moment just to be free of constraint. "As I said, my lord, she is from another time. And it is just her way. She thinks it is humorous."

"Well, I don't, nor will my family. Please consider that when making up the guest list for our breakfast. Or warn her of what is appropriate."

Rachel tried to imagine chastising her grandmother. How would one begin?

"Where would you like to go on our wedding trip?" he said, changing subjects.

Again, she clamped her lips together. That was another thing that infuriated her; when Yarnell was done with a subject he considered it closed, even when she had more to say on the matter. And no amount of trying to reintroduce the topic would work, she had already learned. He was single-minded and obsessive.

"I thought Rome would be lovely," she said.

"Too hot this time of year, and infested with artistic types. You would not like it."

"But I thought . . ."

"No," he said, holding up one hand. "You must accept my word on this, my dear. I have been there and you have not."

And likely never will be, she thought with acerbity. With sudden clarity, she saw her future. After a very short while she would likely be with child—the requisite heir, with luck—and so unfit for travel, and that would be the end of that.

With child!

As much as she knew it was the purpose of their marriage, for Yarnell had never evaded the cold hard fact that he needed an heir, it still gave her the shivers. A girl she had been friends with in childhood had died just the year before in childbirth. Would she be able to express her fears to Yarnell? Would he comfort her? Her mind tripped lightly back to Colin's hug in the hallway, and how for one brief moment she had let her guard down and had been filled with an unwelcome warmth. He had felt so strong and sturdy; comfort flowed from him and through her in waves, and for a few moments all had felt right with the world. Which was all wrong. And so she had drawn away, disturbed by how sheltered she had felt, how protected.

Would Yarnell ever comfort her that way? Make her feel so protected?

Perhaps that would come when they knew each other better. Some day they would be old friends and he would feel free to offer her the little caring gestures that a woman might need on occasion. Not that she was so weak as that. She took in a deep breath. No, she was calm and cool and derived strength from that cold inner core of her that was impermeable to pain.

Yarnell was talking again. "I think a short trip to Wight—we have a summer home there—and then back home. That will be adventurous enough for us. Mother thinks she would like to come along," he finished, casually.

"Your . . . mother is coming on our wedding trip?" she said, her voice rising as she considered the thought. Not only had he never really meant to consult her on where to go—the Wight trip was evidently already planned—but now she had her mother-in-law to contend with on her wedding trip!

"It is her summer home too, Miss Neville, and she will be exhausted once the wedding is over."

His tone was reproving. "Surely you would not deny her the rest and relaxation of her own summer retreat."

"But . . . perhaps we could go elsewhere. Even to your estate. Then your mother would have the Wight summer home to herself."

"No, I think our original plan is best," he said, standing.

Our plan, Rachel thought, hysteria bubbling up. It had never been *her* plan!

"I will take my leave now," he said, bowing to her. "I am happy that this wedding nonsense of your sister's is over so we can commence the planning for our own." He took her hand and laid a circumspect kiss on the glove.

And then he was gone.

Rachel slumped down on the sofa. How had things spun so out of control?

Two

Sir Colin Varens entered the smoky, dim tavern and looked for his contact, a fellow with a hook for a hand. He surveyed the room. Hmm, that presented unexpected difficulties. There were three men with hooks for hands that he could see with a cursory glance, and likely more.

The tavern was old, probably going back three centuries or more, with low-beamed ceilings, tobacco stained with age, and a floor that sagged and moved with every step. They were by the river, and the ineffable stink of the Thames soaked into every timber and every breath of fetid air. He glanced around, looking at each one of the three hooked fellows in turn.

But one of the three was sizing him up, too, and came across the smoky room and grimaced up at him. He was blind in one eye, the film over it making it look like veined marble. "You 'ere ta see Jimmy?"

Colin nodded. That was the name he had been given. "I was told Jimmy was the one who could show me something special." This all seemed silly to him. There was nothing illegal in what he was looking for, after all.

"Foller me, then, mate," the fellow said. He

turned and made his way through the crowd, his rolling gait attesting to his former profession as a seaman. He was now a procurer, of sorts.

As Colin made his way through the room he was uncomfortably aware of the bleary gazes that followed him from many a denizen of the tavern. A girl rubbed up against him and whispered something in his ear. He caught enough to be shocked at her lewd suggestion, and uttered a hasty negative reply. She made a rude gesture. His London sojourn might prove to be an education for him in more ways than one.

His leader pushed open a plank door at the back of the tavern, and led Colin down a dark hallway which opened out to a larger room, equally crowded with men who stood in a circle and cheered, waving chits in the air, smoking and spitting and arguing on occasion. A pall of smoke hung over the crowd, drifting through the yellow light of the lanterns hanging from the beamed ceiling.

"Is this it?" Colin asked.

"Aye. An' mayhap you were expectin' Carlton bloody House?" he said, then roared with laughter at his own jest. He went back the way he had come, leaving Colin alone to find his way through the dense crowd.

Colin stood for a moment, letting his eyes and ears adjust. The gathering was raucous, primarily merry but with moments of dispute between men. Mostly, the gathering seemed to consist of fellows very like his guide, seamen, Thames boatmen. A few he took for barrowmen. Bit by bit he could begin to pick out the better dressed among them. Some were very young gentlemen in expensive jackets, sloshing tankards of the house ale in their hands. Young sprigs of the nobility, no doubt, on a tear and experiencing the seamy underbelly of London life. One or two were being watched by unwholesome chaps willing to relieve them of their gambling money by fair or foul means, Colin was sure. Though he had not been to London in many a year himself, he was too wary and canny a bird to be as incautious as those young fellows.

But apart from the young men, there were others who were a cut above the rest of the crowd, too.

He watched as he began to circle the crowd, and soon, among the hubbub, he picked out three he considered the leaders of this fray.

One gentleman, his face red and choleric and his coat unbuttoned to expose his stout belly, was waving a fist full of banknotes in another's face. It looked one moment as though it would devolve into fisticuffs. Then the next moment the two fellows were pounding one another on the back and laughing uproariously. A sly-looking barmaid swayed up to them at their summons and brought them tankards of ale. The two men clanked the pewter tankards together and drank deeply.

The short, stout fellow's companion was a tall man of advanced age, well-dressed, though not as radiantly attired as the younger fellows, who sported canary waistcoats and a multitude of fobs and were there just for a lark. These gentlemen were here for business.

And still the noise of the crowd shuddered through the rafters, swelled. A final shout rose from the throng as though it was a single entity. Then a hush, and the crowd parted, a burly specimen breaking through, carrying on his back a burden. It was a muscular fellow very much bloodied and beaten, his cut lip swelling and one eye closing up. By the morrow it would likely be black.

Another cheer went up and Colin could see, above the crowd, another fellow lifted on someone's shoulders and paraded around in front of the gathered mass of men, his head almost bunged a couple of times on the low beams. Colin's blood thrummed through his veins. So that was—

"'Ere, you lookin' to get in on the sport, mate?"

A stunted and misshapen gentleman stood before him, a gleam of money-lust in his eyes.

"You mean the betting, I imagine. But no, I am no gambler, sir."

The fellow looked him over, expertly assessing him. "I see," he said, scratching his chin. "Then yer 'ere fer some action. Tell yer what, if yer ready now, you can 'ave a go."

"Who sent you over to me?"

The short man indicated by hooking a thumb over his shoulder the old, well-dressed man, who gazed at Colin with interest and raised his tankard in salute.

This was not what he had expected, but he was indeed here to find some action, and this, apparently, was it. "I'm ready now," Colin said.

"Foine, then." He chuckled, and it was a gurgling, unhealthy sound that ended in a fit of coughing. Flecks of blood were on the fellow's lips when he was done, but he wiped his mouth with the back of his hand and said, "Yer up next. C'mon."

And then, as fast as that, he was in the middle of the crowd, his coat and shirt off, and he faced a bloody giant of a man. Lanterns hanging from the rafters lit the circle of avid faces, some of the men standing on barrels and benches, others crowded in their own tight circles, wagering as they glanced from Colin to his opponent. The smell of sweat and beer and blood was overpowering.

"'E'll never stand up against Mike Lafferty, 'e won't. Look at 'im! Puny," one fellow jeered.

"Aye, but mind, 'e's a moite short, but 'e's fresh; Moike's bin through the wringer with that last bruiser. I'll put a guinea on the new one."

"I'll match that, and give you a tenner 'e won't go the distance. 'E's a greenhorn, not a bruise on 'im!"

Colin shut out the voices and gazed steadily at his opponent. He scuffed his feet in the sawdust on the floor; the finely ground dust was pink with blood and stank of beer foam. This was not home, he realized suddenly, feeling a surge of trepidation. Perhaps he should have waited and watched for a while. He knew every fellow within thirty miles at home. He glanced over at the chap who was nominally in charge.

"You know the rules, lad?"

The man looked him over, and Colin felt he had been assessed and dismissed. He nodded sharply. Too late for second thoughts.

"Then orf you go!"

The shouting immediately started, and the giant circled, his dark eyes gleaming with blood-lust. Colin crouched, put his fists up into the defensive position, and advanced.

And then, as quickly as it began, it was all over.

Colin stared at the ceiling, feeling his jaw swell, the bruising already taking place. So ended his first match in London. It seemed boxing was a little different in London circles.

The day after Pamela's wedding, Rachel sat quietly on a sofa in her fiancé's drawing room. Lady Yarnell, his mother, was spewing a monologue on the benefits of a very abbreviated guest list for the marquess's nuptials. She had just rattled through their own extensive family, naming those who would be invited, those who would not, and those who would be deliberately snubbed. Then she said, as she sewed, "There are so many who have been waiting for so long to see Yarnell wed. He has been the catch of many Seasons, to use the vulgar vernacular. Your family, my dear, I know will want to come, but we must limit it to those who will grace the proceedings with dignity. And we do not want the affair to become too costly, do we? I will tell you whom we believe would be acceptable. I have no objection to your mother, of course, as you well know, and your brother, Lord Haven, would be most welcome. I have heard his new wife spoken of as a very dignified young lady, and would be pleased to improve our brief acquaintance. It was so difficult to do so before you were known to be engaged, and with the hustle and bustle of the Season. Yarnell has told me that she is a very pleasing young woman, and with connections that would not disgrace . . ."

Finally Rachel could no longer hold her silence. "My lady," she said. As her future mother-in-law was looking very startled at being interrupted, Rachel hastened to apologize. "I am so sorry for interrupting, my lady, but I must say that since my mother has been so good as to allow you to put on the wedding breakfast, even though it is her responsibility, in truth, I think that we would like to contribute monetarily. That way we will feel more comfortable inviting all of our family and friends whom we would wish to sit down with us."

Lady Yarnell, her face frozen into a mask of polite disbelief, took in a deep breath, let it out slowly, and said, "I will not take that as an insult, since I feel sure you did not intend it to be."

"I beg your pardon?" Rachel said. "I certainly did not mean any insult, my la . . ."

"However," Lady Yarnell went on, her hand up, palm out, "I am terribly sorry you are so . . . so gauche as to offer money to us. I had been assured by Yarnell that you were well bred. I must now doubt my son's ability to judge, it seems."

The result was a half-hour lecture on the etiquette of weddings and how they were conducted in proper Society. It appeared that Lady Yarnell's idea of this etiquette was solely based on what she wanted and what she did not want. Rachel was resigned, and spent the time gazing around the parlor where they sat together.

This would be her London home, for Yarnell had assured her they would attend each Season, as long as she was able—that was his delicate way of speaking of her being with child—and that he would still come without her when she was no longer able, since he had duties and responsibilities that could be handled only by himself.

The house was so very different from Haven House, her family's London home. Where Haven House was tall and narrow and gloomy, Lord

Yarnell's residence was bright and airy, stately and gleaming with familial pride. The furnishings were cream and white, touched by gilt, and the carpets were thick and plush. And she would soon be mistress of this grand place!

Or at least nominal mistress.

She glanced over at Lady Yarnell again. The woman was still talking. Had Yarnell ever answered her question about his mother and the availability of a dower house for her use? She had the dread premonition that Lady Yarnell would remain as the mistress of Yarnell's home and she would only ever be a sort of guest.

Her musings were brought to an end by the return of Yarnell himself. He entered smiling, a rare expression for him, and after making his obeisance to his mother, he joined Rachel on the sofa. He was a very handsome man, she thought, taking him in in one sweeping side glance before demurely casting her eyes down to her gloved hands again. Dark hair and gray eyes, manly physique, not a blemish or fault to be found, though some might quibble with the cold expression on his face.

But when he smiled, she began to feel some hope of happiness in her future. As man and wife they might think differently, and she might have to sort out the various familial relationships, starting with his austere and masterful mother, but she could do it. This marriage was everything she had set out to accomplish in this Season. She was a lucky young lady.

And she knew it. She was the daughter of a viscount. Yarnell was a marquess, and his family history was old and illustrious, with honors heaped upon accolades.

"I have something for you," he said, with the smile still on his face. "Every prospective groom searches long and hard to find the perfect bride gift for his lady, and I think I have topped them all."

Rachel glanced over at Lady Yarnell, wishing, for once, that the woman would take a hint and leave them alone, as her mother did. But Lady Yarnell was not to be moved. She was sewing, and she continued her long, fine, even line unhindered by any thought that the young people might like a moment in private. She appeared engrossed in her work.

But she was listening. Rachel could tell that. It was in the set of her shoulders and the tilt of her head. She had a feeling that she would come, over the years, to know every minute movement of Lady Yarnell's, and, perhaps, to despise them.

"Have you really?" she said softly to her fiancé, touched by his excitement over finding the perfect gift for her. It attested to the depth of feeling she was sure must truly be there, beneath his frosty demeanor.

"I have." He pulled a box out of his jacket and presented it to her with a flourish. "I hope you like it."

Rachel gazed at the box. Would it be a ring, or a necklace? A locket with a lock of his fine, dark hair? Or even a miniature of himself? She would like that. It would mean that he wanted her to be able to see him and think of him even when he was not present. She slipped the silk ribbon off the box and opened it. Then, with trembling fingers, she pulled away the tissue.

And stared. It was a long, oval, enameled case. She touched the lovely enamel work and the rosette of diamonds that adorned the lid. It was very pretty, but—

"It is a huswife," he said, impatiently.

"I . . . I know." She picked it up. It *was* very pretty, enameled in pink and blue with a scene of a shepherdess and her swain, in a baroque painted frame ornamented by curlicues and roses, each rose centered with a diamond. She opened it. In the lid was a thimble, and the case itself was cunningly fitted with tiny scissors, a folding fruit knife, a set of needles and other implements. "Th-thank you my lord."

He frowned. "Do you not like it?"

Tears starting in her eyes, she looked up at him. A set of sewing implements. That was his idea of a good wedding gift for her. She sighed deeply and felt the tears spill over. Let him think it was the emotion of the moment. "I am overcome, my lord," she said, simply, and he was satisfied.

"I knew it would be perfect," he said. "Now I have to leave again. I have some very important business to attend to."

Three

Andromeda Varens and Belinda de Launcey sat at the breakfast table planning their day over toast and marmalade. Andromeda glanced up over her glasses and watched thirteen-year-old Belinda drinking coffee, an unanticipated privilege and one of the many reasons she said she liked being with her new friend. *You are so unexpected,* the child had said one day. What exactly that meant, Andromeda was not sure.

True, she had made friends among many different circles of people since descending upon London: the literati, the theater folk, and even a dedicated circle of bird-watchers who were planning a foray into the countryside to view, variously, the chaffinch, willow warbler, and the reed bunting. And it was also true that she had a different sense of humor from most of the folks in her circle, finding amusement in the most serious of subjects at times. Inappropriate, her laughter had been called, but so be it. She was beginning to think she had bowed to societal pressure for far too long, keeping herself stiff and correct when she really wanted a bit of fun.

She had finally confessed to herself—the shock of spending time in London after many years isolated in Yorkshire speeding her voyage of self-discovery—that she was not the grand lady she had fancied herself while in her insular Yorkshire society. In the sparsely populated environs of Lesleydale, she was second only to the Neville ladies in consequence. Here she was much lower in status, and would have to humble herself, if she wanted to clamber up to a better level of Society, by becoming a bootlicking sycophant, not a role she would willingly take on. The second shock was finding out she did not care to attain that hypothetical higher status. She liked who she was, not who she thought she should be. Salutary lesson, that.

Belinda was drinking coffee, humming, reading a book, and eating toast with Seville marmalade as she kicked restlessly at the table leg in a most unladylike way. The girl missed her uncle, but she had been kind enough to say that Andromeda was a 'smashing substitute'! Andromeda treated her as an adult most of the time, and perhaps that was a novel experience.

Glancing back down at her notebook, Andromeda bit her lip. "Belinda, do you think it would be too shocking if you went backstage with me at Mr. Lessington's theater Wednesday evening?"

No answer.

Looking up from her notebook, glasses down on her nose, Andromeda said, "Belinda! Did you not hear a word I said? I asked if you thought it would be too shocking if you went backstage with me at Mr. Lessington's theater Wednesday evening."

"It wouldn't be shocking at all," Belinda answered.

"*You* wouldn't think so, would you? And even if

you did, you would not admit it." Andromeda
replied, dryly. She gazed at the girl with affection.
If she had ever been blessed with a child, she
would have liked a girl like Belinda, up to any rig,
fun-loving, smart. But at thirty-one, she supposed
her wishes would never bear fruit, nor would her
body. And with Haven married now—she abandoned that old hurt and glared down at her
notebook. She had really loved her old neighbor,
the playmate of her youth, with a kind of desperate love that had made her do embarrassing things
she would just as soon forget. But he was married
now, and try as she might she could not dislike his
wife, Jane, the new Lady Haven. She had wondered lately if her love for Haven had been more
for who he once was than for who he was now.

But all of that, the hopes and dreams of a giddy
girl, were behind her now. At her age, Andromeda felt she had lost whatever youthful attraction
she had had. She had never been a pretty girl,
and now was too bony and hard, she feared, to attract anyone but a fellow desperate for a wealthy
wife, and she would never stoop to the advances
of a fortune hunter. She was wealthy in her own
right, with more actual available money than her
brother, as a result of her late maternal grandmother's legacy. She could purchase a husband
and no one would think the worse of her for it,
but long ago had decided that would never do
for her. She would just resign herself to staying
husbandless.

Oh, but how she would have liked a daughter.
She looked up and smiled at Belinda's eager expression. The idea of going backstage at the
theater had been canvassed before, but An-

dromeda would need to be sure nothing truly shocking was going on before she allowed it. She had only a vague idea, but she had heard that sometimes the actresses were . . . she shied away from her scandalous musings. "Well, we shall see. First, I am not sure that the play at Mr. Lessington's theater is suitable viewing for one of your impressionable age. We may have to go to another theater. I would do nothing to alarm your uncle, even if he might learn of it too late to prevent it from taking place."

"My uncle is the one who allowed me to ride in breeches astride in Hyde Park!" Belinda, claimed, stoutly.

"That was because he was besotted with Pamela," Andromeda said, about Strongwycke's new wife, her old friend Miss Pamela Neville. "He would have done anything for love of her." She sighed deeply, wondering what it was like to have a man so in love with you as that. She had never experienced it.

At that moment, Colin limped into the breakfast room.

"What on earth has happened to you?" Andromeda said, rising from her chair and hastening to her younger brother's side.

He held out one hand to ward her off. "Leave off, Andy," he said, irritably.

He took a seat at the round breakfast table and signaled to the footman, garbed in Strongwycke's family colors of buff and rust, for coffee.

Belinda stared at him and Andromeda examined his face. His jaw was dark, bruised along the bone line. He winced as he drank the hot coffee, then sighed and sat back in the chair. Becoming aware of their scrutiny, he said, "Just a little dustup, that's all!"

Her voice trembling, Andromeda said, "This was no tavern fight, brother. You have been boxing again, haven't you?"

He shrugged. "It's *my* life, Andy, in case you have forgotten. There is nothing wrong with boxing. It is a sport, just like fencing or riding."

"Except in fencing you do not run your opponent through," she said. She fought down her anger. It was fear, and she knew its genesis: more than one man had been killed in the ring, to her knowledge, even in their confined Yorkshire community. How much more dangerous would it be in London? In Lesleydale, Colin was accounted a fair bruiser, but one did not need to know London to be able to figure out that there would be many bigger, harder, more capable men in so large a society. Colin was in real danger.

"You listen to me, little brother," she said, waggling one long, bony finger in his face. "I will not have you killing yourself in some ring because you have been unsuccessful in love!"

He flushed and glanced at Belinda. "Don't tell me what to do, Andy. I am my own man, and I do not box out of some insane desire to be beaten. Nor am I pining away from unsuccessful love, not for Pammy, nor for . . . for Rachel."

Belinda was pretending not to hear, intent on the book she had in her hands, but Andromeda knew she was listening and didn't care. The girl was family, or practically so, anyway. "If this is the result of your first London bout, then I would say it is a fair indication you are outclassed," she said, indicating his bruised jaw. "*And* you are limping."

"That is because of the way I fell. I just need some practice. I am going to find this fellow, this boxing trainer I have heard of. I won't go into my next match unprepared, like I did this one." He sipped his coffee and grimaced.

"You will not box again, do you hear me?" She heard her voice, the hysteria rising like tidewater. Taking a deep breath, she sat down in the chair next to him and examined his bruises. His face had never been pretty; he had a low-slung jaw and a beaky nose, and his hair was a tumble of careless curls. With the bruising he looked even worse, like a low-class street fighter. But she loved him just the same, and had since the moment she had first seen him as a tiny, squalling, red-faced baby. She remembered that moment with great clarity, even though she had been only three herself. Their mother had presented the baby boy newly brought into the world for his big sister's examination and she, in her baby mind, had thought of him as a gift for her. From that moment forward, she had protected him whenever she could, and feared for him when she couldn't.

But he would recover . . . this time. Forcing a note of calm into her voice, she said, "Colin, it is one thing in Yorkshire to box the local fellows because you are bored, but there is so much more to do in London! It is alive with culture and entertainment. Why do you not come to the theater with me, or . . . or to the bookstore!"

"You have your interests and I have mine. I do not tell you to leave off watching birds fly around to come and see a boxing match, do I?"

"At least my interests are civilized," she

snapped. "I do not understand why men need to beat each other senseless and then call it sport."

"You will never understand." A footman brought a wet cloth to Colin, and he applied it to his bruised chin, giving a deep sigh of relief. "Thank you, James," he said, looking up at the footman, who was concealing a grin behind his mask of a perfect servant's blank expression. "I can tell you have likely done this a time or two yourself, my lad."

Andromeda stood and indicated to Belinda to follow. "No, I will never understand. And I will never condone what you do. It is brutal and uncivilized, and you must be mad."

"I am a man, Andy. Ladies have been accusing us of brutality for eons. At least this brutality is focused upon each other."

She glared down at him. "If you are trying to be humorous, you are falling flat. Come, Belinda, we have a *brilliant* day ahead of us. We are going to make the most of what this marvelous city has to offer." Her head lifted high, she swept from the room.

Rachel was just beginning to realize how much she missed her brother and especially her younger sister, Pamela. She had not been the best sister, she thought, for many years now. But lately, she had felt closer again to Pamela, though that was cut short by her sister's marriage and departure. It was almost as though she had been in a deep freeze for years, like ice at the bottom of the deepest moorland caverns, and for some reason was beginning to thaw. She was not sure that was a good thing. Frozen, one never could be hurt. But this London Season had seen many changes in her, and had forced her to confront many truths.

Primary among them was that this advantageous marriage she had agreed to would not make of life a picnic. There would be a price to pay for the prize, and the bill was coming due even before she received the goods.

It was a lovely spring Tuesday afternoon, and yet instead of walking in the park, as she would like to be doing, she was forced to immure herself in the gloomy depths of Haven House. Lady Yarnell had made the necessary visit to her prospective in-laws' residence in the company of her sister, and Rachel's mother and grandmother were present as well. They were sitting in the best drawing room, and even though it had recently been refurbished to some extent, it was still gloomy and awkward and dingy. All in all, it was as uncomfortable a meeting as one could imagine.

Rachel sat alone on a sofa, staring out the window. Spring through the high window looked like a glorious, misty painting viewed from a Stygian gallery. The palette outside was green and blue; inside, all was gray and brown. Her mother and grandmother were seated in hard, high-backed chairs opposite the other ladies. Ostensibly they were to talk of wedding arrangements, but they had not reached that point yet.

Lady Yarnell's sister was widow of an admiral lost in the wars off the coast of Spain. Lady Beaufort appeared haughty, but today she was making a concerted effort to ease the discomfort of the gathering by chattering about gossip: who was new to London, who was leaving, what scandal was just being hinted at in the papers.

Lady Haven, Rachel's mother, who had at first seemed afraid of Lord Yarnell's mother, appeared to be exceedingly put out by the other woman's manner, and was making up to Lady Beaufort. It was a frosty little confrontation, as Lady Beaufort mediated between the groom-to-be's mother and the bride-to-be's mother, trying to lead them both into pleasant conversation. Grandmother, for once, was holding her tongue. Rachel could only pray that continued.

She was grateful for the appearance of more company, even if it was just Miss Andromeda Varens, with whom she had not gotten along for many years now, and Belinda de Launcey, Strongwycke's headstrong, impulsive niece. "It is so good to see you both," she cried, rising, and was ashamed to see how surprised Andromeda was by her pleasant greeting.

But, not one to hold a grudge, Miss Varens led Belinda to the sofa as Rachel sat back down; they took a seat beside her after being introduced to the rest of the gathering. Rachel was so relieved to see Andromeda's familiar face that she felt quite in charity with the other woman for perhaps the first time in years.

"How are you enjoying your London stay?" Rachel asked, aiming the question at both the younger and the older lady.

Belinda was silent, merely shrugging an answer. Andromeda cast her a questioning glance, but then turned and said to Rachel, "I am enjoying it far more than I anticipated. I came, originally, just to purchase books for the ladyschool at Lesleydale, you know, but now that I'm here I'm finding much more to enjoy than I thought I would. Either London has improved or I have become more tolerant."

"Have you been to the theater lately?" asked Rachel, prompted by a sudden impulse. "We are going tomorrow night, and I would be so pleased if you would join us."

"I shall have to converse with Colin to see what he has planned," Andromeda said, hesitantly. "We did intend to go to the theater tomorrow night, but I have not seen about a box yet."

"He is welcome, too," Rachel said, desperately. She felt the need for someone who was unequivocally on her side. Her mother and grandmother had a previous engagement, and it would be just her, Lord Yarnell, and his mother, otherwise. "Yarnell very kindly told me that if I had any acquaintance, I might invite them when the box was not full."

"As long as we would not be in the way," Andromeda said, her tone nettled.

"No, not at all . . . I mean . . ." For the first time, Rachel realized how she sounded. It must have seemed as if the invitation was extended only because there was no one better to invite. "No," she said, putting out one hand and placing it on Andromeda's wrist. "I would deem it a favor and an honor if you all would join us," she said.

Her gaunt face relaxing, her expression warming, Andromeda still hesitated. "Would . . . would Belinda be allowed to come? I have promised her a trip to the theater, as I said, and . . ."

"Of course she will be welcome," Rachel said. "Both as your friend and as family to me, in a sense. After all, she is my brother-in-law's niece, and so, by extension, mine, too. We are going to the Libris Theater, and they are having a comedy, very light, very suitable." She met the girl's eyes and said, "Would you come, Miss de Launcey? I would be so pleased."

Overwhelmed by this notice from someone who had ignored her existence until now, Belinda eagerly nodded. "I would like that."

"Good, then it is settled." Rachel paused and listened to the other ladies for a moment. The conversation seemed to be flowing rather better, due entirely to Lady Beaufort's efforts, and she relaxed. She turned to her guests. "I am so happy you're finding London to your liking. It is vastly different from home, isn't it?"

Andromeda said, grimly, "Yes, though some things are the same." She clamped her lips shut and reddened.

"Is . . . is anything wrong?"

Belinda, bursting with a desire to impart something of interest, leaned forward, her eyes shining. "Miss Varens is so very upset! You see, Sir Colin has been beaten to within an inch of his life."

Four

"What? I beg your pardon?" Rachel felt a strange, sick jolt under her ribcage. "How did this happen?" Her hands trembled and she clamped them together on her lap. "Was he way-laid by robbers? Is he all right? Miss Varens, surely you would have said something immediately if his condition was grave!"

Andromeda gave her a penetrating look, and even her grandmother's basilisk gaze swiveled in Rachel's direction at the panic in her voice. She deliberately tamped down her alarm, forcing herself to sit calmly, hands folded together in her lap. She toyed with the blue silk ribbons that adorned her aqua day gown, finding she could not, after all, be perfectly still.

"Belinda is overstating the case," Andromeda said, with a warning glance at her young charge. "Colin is just fine, Miss Neville. He is bruised and limping, but I do not think any real damage is done."

"But what . . ."

The older woman looked around, and, finally satisfied that the others were intent on their own conversation, she leaned forward as if she had a shameful secret to impart. "He has been boxing again," she said. She sat back up and clamped her lips shut into a prim line. Her violet-hued turban hat slipped just a little, and she put one hand up to steady it, then affixed it better on her pomaded curls.

"Again? What do you mean? Boxing? *Colin?*" Rachel frowned, trying to understand this strange new view of her old friend and many times rejected suitor, Colin. He had always been gentle, tender, even meek with her, and though she did not want to marry him, and had told him so in no uncertain terms—sometimes quite rudely, she was ashamed to admit—he had retained his exquisite manners. As countrified as he was—and he appeared even more so set against the backdrop of London beaux and dandies—he still was mild to a fault, considerate and careful.

And she was to believe that man was a boxer?

His sister shrugged helplessly. "Men! At home he is considered the best fighter in the neighboring villages. He has been beaten only rarely. I have looked the other way for a long time now, though I have known about his . . . *sport* for many years. I knew he had his . . . frustrations and needed an outlet for his manly vigor."

Frustrations. Andromeda was delicately speaking of his futile pursuit of her. Rachel stiffened, ready to defend her determined rejection of Colin with an explicit explanation, if necessary.

"Not that you . . . or anyone," Andromeda continued, hastening back into speech, her gaunt cheeks blazing with color, "should have done anything differently. Hearts will go where they will go, and I well know there is no forcing . . . in short, one cannot make oneself feel what one does not."

It was an awkward little speech, but it was meant, Rachel knew, to excuse her of any purposeful cruelty to Colin. And since Andromeda loved her brother fiercely—everyone knew that, despite her odd manner—it was nobly and kindly done. Andromeda was excusing her from wrongdoing, Colin was a boxer of some repute . . . everything, even the room around her seemed strange, unfamiliar. Her world had shifted a little. She had been so convinced she knew the people in her small home circle, and yet they could still surprise her. What else did she not know? Must she question everything that had seemed firm and fixed?

London was proving to hold surprises that had nothing to do with the city itself or those who lived there.

"In short, I have winked at his brutal sport until now," Andromeda continued. "He is reputed to be the best in Yorkshire," she said, with something that *seemed* almost like pride, if one did not know how she abhorred the sometimes barbarous sport. "But London . . ." She shook her head, her expression dark and doubtful. "I am so worried. He has been in only one bout, last night, and he was beaten, from what I understand, likely on the first punch. So now he says he is going to some fellow for training, probably some low brute from the docks."

Rachel shuddered. "Boxing!" She knew little about it but what she had heard whispered among some of the younger fellows in the ballrooms. "That is so rough, coarse even, like bear-baiting. I can't believe that Colin would take part in something so . . . so squalid."

"But I have seen a bout," Belinda said, moving

forward to the edge of her seat, "and it is really quite thrilling!"

Both women looked at her with wide eyes.

"What are you talking about?" Andromeda demanded. "You have seen a bout? How is that possible?"

Belinda's cheeks were pink, but she nodded, her eyes shining. She wriggled in her seat like a puppy, and said, "I . . . well, I ran away from school last autumn—Uncle Strongwycke was not best pleased, I can tell you, but I was upset about things—and I made my way back almost all the way to Shadow Manor. But I stopped and begged for employment at a tavern as a . . . I, uh, helped in the kitchen." She frowned and shook her head. "I thought it would be romantic to work as some other girls do, but it was horrid, never enough to eat, tired all the time . . . I was only there a few days, but it was hideous. Anyway, one night in the back room the tavern owner made me take ale to the men." She shuddered. "You would not believe the smell of that place! Anyway, they were boxing, and I watched. You have never seen anything like it; it truly is thrilling in a savage kind of way."

"What could possibly be thrilling in watching two men beat each other senseless? That is base bestiality, just like any tavern brawl," Andromeda said, dismissing Belinda's observations.

Rachel saw the quick hurt in the girl's eyes, and remembered being thirteen and having her opinions dismissed as if she did not have a brain. Every female suffered the same thing for most of her life, but as a child it was harder to bear because one began to believe that one had nothing of value to add to a conversation. As a woman, one came to understand it was just the way of the world, or the way of men, anyway, and of little relation to one's true intelligence. "What do you think made it so very thrilling?" she asked the girl.

Belinda turned gratefully to Rachel. "Well, it was not just two men beating each other, as you would think. One could see them first circling each other, sizing the other up. And then one would feint and the other would parry, just like fencing, only with their bare fists! And all the while the tension is building. And then there comes a moment when everything seems to pause—time itself appears to stop—and then the fight begins in earnest."

"I still say it is barbaric, brutish, and cruel, no sport at all, but just mindless pummeling." Andromeda harrumphed and flounced, her girlish skirts and ruffles bouncing with the movement.

Rachel could not but say, "I have to agree with Andromeda. It sounds appallingly bestial, and I cannot imagine what, in such brutality, Colin finds appealing."

At that moment Lady Beaufort and Lady Yarnell rose and said good-bye to Lady Haven and the dowager. Lady Yarnell, still with the same frosty and forbidding manner, said, "So, it is set. You will visit Friday, and we will make some arrangements for the wedding." She put out her hand and Lady Haven took it.

Rachel was watching and saw the dislike in her mother's eyes. Oh dear, this was going to be awkward, this wedding business. Then Lady Yarnell motioned to Rachel. "Miss Neville, would you walk us out, please?"

Rachel looked longingly back to Andromeda

and Belinda. She had been interested in their conversation and, strangely, wanted to hear more about Colin and his barbarous sport. But she knew her duty and followed her future mother-in-law.

"Miss Neville," Lady Yarnell said, as they walked through the dank hall to the front door, "who was that . . . *lady* and child who came in, and with whom you were carrying on such an . . . animated conversation."

Rachel, irritated by Lady Yarnell's implied disapproval—she did it all with the hesitations in her speech—said, "That is Miss Andromeda Varens, sister to the baronet Sir Colin Varens and a close neighbor of ours at home; with her was Miss Belinda de Launcey, my brother-in-law's orphaned niece. Miss Varens has stayed in London at Lord Strongwycke's home to take care of the child while my sister and her husband travel north on their nuptial trip."

"And why is the gel not at school, or at the very least in the nursery with a governess?"

"I am quite sure that is none of my affair, my lady," Rachel said, and was distracted by a snort from Lady Beaufort, who sounded like she had just swallowed an insect. A quick glance sufficed to assure Rachel that the lady was fine, though she was stifling some expression. It almost looked like amusement.

Lady Yarnell's countenance closed like a shutter, her eyes hooded, her mouth prim. "I do hope those . . . *parvenus*—this baronet and his sister—are not some of the people you would like to come to our wedding."

Our wedding? Rachel felt a rising tide of anger,

but suppressed it, stuffing it back down like a recalcitrant gown into a trunk.

"Sister," Lady Beaufort said, "a baronet, his sister, and the niece of an earl can hardly be considered parvenus!"

"They can by a marquess." Lady Yarnell whirled, started down the front steps, then turned at the door of her carriage, an ancient but respectable landau. "Regardless, one can tell just by looking at Miss Varnish, or whatever her name is—that foolish, girlish mode of dress, that odd turban she wore—that she is never going to be good *ton*. I would be just as happy never to see her again. Good day, Miss Neville. I look forward to the theater tomorrow night. We shall speak of this further at that time."

Lady Beaufort threw back an apologetic look, but followed her sister without comment to the waiting carriage.

Rachel stood as the butler closed the door and stared at the blank wooden door. Lady Yarnell did not know that she had invited Andromeda and Belinda to the theater. She felt a queasy sickness in her stomach. She knew from listening to some of her acquaintance that one's husband's mother could make a new wife's life a misery or a joy. Men had their own world and their own life away from the home, but a woman, especially once she began breeding, was confined to the home a great deal of the time. If Lady Yarnell took her in dislike, it could be a long, long while before she was able to feel comfortable in her marriage.

She turned back and slowly walked toward the drawing room. She would have to retract her invitation. How could she do that? She would just have to. She took a deep breath and entered, re-joining her two guests. Her mother and grandmother were deep in conversation together, oddly. That happened rarely, since the two did not generally get along.

As she sat down on the sofa, Andromeda put out one hand and touched Rachel's. "My dear, you do not look quite well. Are you all right?"

"I am fine, I thank you for your concern." She swallowed. "I find . . . I find I must r-retract my invitation to the theater tomorrow night. I have just been informed by her ladyship that . . . that Lady Yarnell has company, and that her theater box will be quite full."

Andromeda's expression told of her disappointment. "Oh. That is unfortunate. Well, you cannot help that, Miss Neville. Some other time."

Miserably aware that there would never be a next time, not with Lady Yarnell's feelings so clearly expressed, Rachel nodded.

"But we must leave," Andromeda said. "We have a full afternoon ahead. We are going to Hatchards, and then there is to be a balloon elevation in the park and I have promised Belinda we shall watch." She stood and put out her hand. "I must say, we have had a pleasant visit."

Rachel took her gloved hand. Their afternoon sounded like so much fun! She had to stay in, since they were expecting a visit from a superior seamstress who was going to interview them to see if she wanted to concoct Rachel's wedding gown. "I'm sure you will have a splendid day. I . . . you will tell me if Colin is all right?"

"I am sure he is," Andromeda replied, examining Rachel's face with her piercing gaze.

Rachel, flustered, then offered her hand to Belinda de Launcey. "It has been a pleasure, Miss de Launcey."

Belinda dropped a curtsy, and thanked her.

They left, and Rachel slumped down on the sofa.

"Rachel," her grandmother said, her strident voice echoing in the high-ceilinged drawing room. "Why does that fatheaded, overbearing witch, whose name I shall never say in my remaining lifetime, short as that may be, but who is to become your mother-in-law, not like me and why is she trying to dissuade me from coming to your wedding?"

Rachel felt the tears come. Blink them back as she might, they would not stop. For once she had reason to be glad the room was so gloomy, even on a brilliant spring day. She sniffed them back, but they would keep coming. When had her wedding gotten so out of her own control? And how could she wrest back any vestige of authority?

And why did everything seem like such a dreary chore when she had achieved her life's goal?

What was she going to do?

Five

He would never suffer another humiliation like the one the night before, Colin decided. His mistake had been one of ignorance; he had never considered that Yorkshire and London were very different venues when it came to his favorite sport. Colin was determined to learn all there was to learn about boxing in London. He was at the door of the Apollonian Club and took a deep breath, looking up at the façade, an expanse of gold brick. The doors were enormous oak slabs with brass hinges and gilt lettering with the club name and a radiant sun in highly polished brass. Inside was the gentleman he had been told could change his luck—or, rather, refine his skill—in the boxing ring. He must find a way to convince him, though, to take on a new protégé, for the fellow was notoriously particular about those with whom he associated.

Colin climbed the scrubbed steps, entered, and spoke to the club manager. The man assessed him, looking over his country clothing, and then considered his manner and speech as they talked. There was nothing quite like being judged by a London club manager and found wanting.

"I'm sorry, sir, but the gentleman you wish to speak to . . ."

Colin had one name to give, and that was a school friend of his with whom he had kept in contact, and who had told him to look him up at the Apollonian if he ever got to London. He gave that name and said, "He said to feel free to visit the Apollonian if I should get down to London."

That name was the magic key that unlocked the door, surmounting even objections over his countrified appearance, and Colin was allowed past the manager's desk and into the sanctity of the club as a guest. He happened to know his friend was abroad at that moment, but that did not matter. He clearly had the right connections.

Thank the Lord for old school friends, Colin thought as he glanced around at the plush interior, done in muted shades of gold and red. Many doors opened off a central gallery, and from his friend's description there would be, among others, a reading room, a gambling room, and rooms upstairs kept for the member's convenience while in town.

The man for whom he searched would not be in the gambling rooms, so he ignored the high shouts of laughter and low murmur of conversation that came with club gaming, and headed for what appeared to be the reading room, a quiet cool den furnished with chairs, tables, and all the London papers, as well as a few select journals from those foreign countries in which a gentleman could be expected to be interested.

Colin had an excellent description, so when he saw the fellow, he immediately knew it was him.

Lucky on his first foray! That had to be a good omen.

Sauntering over to the deep club chair, Colin surreptitiously examined the man sitting and reading the *Times*. He was of middle years, lean and dark of visage, his skin the color of fine leather. It attested to the man's time in the tropics and to his occupation as a planter in the Caribbean. He had a high, beaky nose and light blue eyes, so pale they looked almost clear. If the man was aware of his intense scrutiny, he was deliberately ignoring him.

Colin took a deep breath, rubbed his palms against his thighs, and said, "Sir Parnell Waterford?"

The man turned pale eyes on him and raised his graying brows. "Yes? What can I do for you, young fellow?"

He hadn't intended to blurt it out, but he did anyway. "You can teach me to box."

"And why would I do that?"

Colin indicated the other chair and raised his eyebrows, but the fellow just watched him, with no indication of invitation. Nettled, Colin dropped into the chair anyway. "I hear, sir, that you are, next to Gentleman Jackson, the man to see in London about boxing."

Waterford rattled his paper and resumed reading, crossing his long legs in front of him as he leaned back at his ease.

Stunned by the blatant rudeness, Colin sat for a moment without reacting, and then snatched the paper away from the older man, saying, "Sir, at least do me the common courtesy of listening to me when I speak to you." He tossed the paper aside, out of reach.

Waterford sat up straight and stared steadily at Colin for a moment, his gaze traveling Colin's bruised jawline before meeting the younger man's eyes again. There might have been a twinkle in the depths of his odd eyes. "Would it not behoove you to introduce yourself, sir, before you so rudely make demands on my time? And I would have you know from the onset, by the way, that if you are only coming to me because you have been rejected as a candidate of the Gentleman's tutelage, you will find me a poor substitute. We do not have the same methods, and I do not take anyone on who would pay for their lessons elsewhere."

Puzzled, Colin stuck out his hand, and gave his name, his home county, and then said, "Sir, I have not been to Gentleman Jackson's at all. He will teach anyone with the coin. I heard that you were the one who could teach a fellow, but only if you believed he had promise."

"Why does that matter?"

"I am not a dilettante, sir. I really am very good."

"Then why do you need me?"

Colin fingered his bruised jaw. He frowned and stared off through the smoky reading room toward a curtained window, draped in deep red velvet. "I know I am good, but I don't know anything about London, how the matches are run, who the fighters are, what I might expect. Also, I lack a certain . . . finesse in the ring, I fear. Things here are different than in Yorkshire. It would take too long to learn through trial and error, and I have only a month or so."

"And why do you want to box? You are a gentleman and therefore, presumably, an amateur. Surely you should be content to bet on the professionals, as most gentlemen do, and be satisfied with sparring occasionally with other gentlemen pugilists?"

"I am not a gambler." Colin shrugged and met the other man's gaze. "I am not a gambler, I'm a boxer, and, as I said, no dilettante. I like it. I'm good at it. It doesn't really matter my class, does it?"

"You cannot expect to be as good as the men who depend upon it for their livelihood. You don't have enough at stake." Waterford again crossed one ankle over the other and sat back in his chair, his eyes never leaving Colin's face.

"With or without your training, I will fight. I can't explain it. Some men paint, others compose music, and others . . . others build their whole life around their clothes and jewelry," he said, bitterly, thinking of Lord Yarnell and his perfection of dress and manner. "I fight."

"I take no money."

"Good. I have very little to give."

"I am a stern taskmaster."

"And I a dedicated student."

Waterford stood, straightening his lanky limbs, and put out his hand. "Then let us see if we can make you a better fighter, Sir Colin!"

Bounding to his feet and shaking the older man's hand vigorously, Colin said, "You mean you'll take me on?"

The knight put up one cautioning hand. "First things first. I'll see what you have, then decide. How about that?"

"That's fair. That's more than fair."

"Then let us go back to my rooms. I have a place set up and my manservant, Roger—he used to box until his eye went bad—acts as a sparring partner. We shall see if you'll do."

Colin nodded sharply. All he needed was this one opportunity.

"I'm *glad* we're not stuck in some stuffy box, Miss Varens," Belinda de Launcey said, her arm through her friend's. "One can't truly experience the theater sitting in some segregated box."

"Kind of you to say, my dear, since there were no boxes available on such short notice." They were pulled apart by the buffeting of the crowd, but Andromeda firmly grasped Belinda's wrist and pulled her back, putting her arm over the girl's shoulders. "If we had gone to Mr. Lessington's theater he would have found us a spot, I have no doubt, but his troupe is not mounting anything suitable at the moment. And I truly wanted to see *this* play." Andromeda glanced around her nervously. "However, I have not been to the Season in so very long, I forgot what a tangle it is at this time of year."

It was Wednesday evening, and they were making their way through the rude crowds. Andromeda was having second and even third thoughts about the advisability of having young Miss de Launcey with her. It would have been different in a box, where they would have been secure from the impatient crowd. And when one had a box, one was treated infinitely better by the serving staff and everyone else. It had likely not been wise to bring a thirteen-year-old girl with her without the security of a box seat.

Although, from some of the tales the girl had told, Belinda was up to any rig. Andromeda, of course, would never praise her thus to her face. Notwithstanding the use of low cant, which she never indulged in, she also did not think it was wise to praise behavior that could well get the girl in deep trouble.

A skinny man swayed and fell in front of them in the narrow aisle as they tried to fight their way to some seat—a drunken sot, no doubt—and it was just too much. She had not intended to come alone with Belinda, but Colin had not been back all day, and finally, after some persuading from her young friend, she had decided they could go alone. But this was too much. Andromeda turned and tugged at Belinda. "Come, this is too crowded. I never should have thought of such a mad scheme. I will not have you subjected to this any longer."

"Miss Varens! Please . . . look, there are some seats over there, and a very gentlemanly looking man seated. Let us sit by him."

Andromeda pulled her shawl tightly around her shoulders, clutched her umbrella to her bosom, and bit her lip. She looked down at Belinda's eager face, shining with anticipation, and then gazed around her. The crowd was settling somewhat. The house lights were going down and the stage gaslights were going up, flaring and popping as the gas hissed.

"All right," she said, suddenly. She grasped her young companion's hand and they made their way between the benches down to the empty spaces, pushing past people's knees, tripping over baskets of food and wine. She stopped boldly before the man and said, "Sir, do you mind if we sit by you?"

He looked them over, his eyes glittering strangely, but his voice was mannerly enough as he said, "Certainly, madam. Please have a seat."

The play was engrossing at first. Not liking the look of the fellow on the other side of the empty space, Andromeda had put Belinda between herself and the polite gentleman. After the first half hour of the play, the man next to her began to lean heavily against her, and soon he was asleep, snoring loudly in her ear. She tried shoving him back, and her turban became dislodged and anchored over one eye. She fought with it, and managed to get it back on top of her head.

Belinda was squirming for some unknown reason, and Andromeda was finding it increasingly uncomfortable. She began to regret such a harebrained scheme and thought that perhaps they ought to leave. But there was no going, with it as dark as it was in the pit seating area.

She glanced around, peering through the gloom. They were a good ways from the aisle. It would take a while and cause a commotion if they were to leave. When she turned back it was to see Belinda, her face frozen in distaste or something worse, leaning away from the man on the other side of her.

"What is wrong, Belinda? Are you not enjoying the play?"

Her mouth trembling, the girl whispered, her voice a moan of fear, "Miss Varens, he keeps trying to . . . trying to touch me!"

Andromeda, shocked to her very core, bent over and stared at the man on the other side of her companion, to find the man's hand on Belinda's knee. Without another thought, she balled her fist and hit him in the general region of his stomach, or somewhat lower, and the man doubled over.

"What's wrong with you?" he hollered, and even over the chatter in the audience and the loud voices of the actors declaiming on stage, it could be heard. "You brought the little whore to be sold. I just want a sample of her wares!"

Andromeda leaped to her feet and beat the man with the umbrella she had brought with her as protection against the misty weather. Then, as the fracas became general, she hauled Belinda to her feet and they stumbled and staggered away from the fray as the serving staff hurriedly lit the house lights, and large men employed to keep calm descended on the scene.

Belinda stopped. Her face was turned up and she was staring above them. Andromeda was forced to follow suit. There, in a box, was Rachel Neville, her fiancé, and Lady Yarnell in their safe, sequestered box. And with not another soul in sight, even though it was well into the first act. Their eyes were on the melee, though, and they did not see the two gazing up at them.

Until Rachel looked down into the pits.

Andromeda paused only a moment as her eyes met Rachel's. Then she pulled Belinda behind her as they exited the theater, the commotion rising in volume behind them as they made their way through the passage and out to the night, looking for a carriage.

* * *

"What kind of an idiot would take a child to a theater and sit in the pit?" Andromeda paced, her frilly skirts flying out behind her as her large feet clumped on the uncarpeted hardwood floor of the Strongwycke mansion drawing room. She whirled and dropped at Belinda's feet. "Oh, my dear child," she said, hugging her again for about the third or fourth time. "I am so sorry I took you there! And you were subjected to that . . . that filthy lecher's groping!"

"Miss Varens, we survived. I am just fine, believe me!" Belinda was curled up in a chair with her night rail and robe on and a cup of hot chocolate at her elbow. Her dark tresses had been combed and washed, losing all smell of the smoky, dirty, beer-drenched theater.

The clock struck midnight, and Andromeda dropped into a chair and covered her face with her hands, groaning. "And now it is midnight, and you are still up, and no one in their right mind would keep a thirteen-year-old girl up this late. Oh, what a wretched mother I would have made. God knew what He was doing when He saw fit to keep me without husband and children."

"But that is not true," Belinda cried. "You would have made a smashing mother. Look what adventures we have had!"

The vast drawing room door creaked open and Colin limped in, his homely face drawn and weary.

"Where have you been?" Andromeda said, uncovering her eyes and glaring at him, her tone acerbic.

He frowned, crossed to the decanters sitting on

a tray on a table, and poured himself some port. "I have had the most amazing evening, Andy. I met a man . . ." He stopped as he took in the scene, his glass half way to his mouth. "I say, why is Miss de Launcey still up? Don't children generally go to bed with the sun?"

"I am not a child," Belinda said. She put her mug of chocolate down with a slam on the table.

Andromeda sighed and shook her head. "Oh, Colin," she groaned. "I am unfit to have her here at all! I must write her uncle to come and get her, for I . . ."

"No! Miss Varens, please don't send me away!"

Colin sat in a chair and looked at the two of them, finally sensing, perhaps, the anxiety of his sister. "What's wrong? What has happened?"

Andromeda told him the whole tale, and at first Colin was amused, until she got to the part about the groping stranger, the fight, and their flight from the theater.

"This is my fault," he said running his knobby fingers through his tousled hair. "I have been sadly remiss and I apologize to you both. I have been a selfish beast, Andy. You should have told me so." He leaped to his feet, hugged his sister briefly, fiercely, and took Belinda's hand, squeezing it. "I will do better. We shall go to the theater, and I will make sure we have a box. I may have acquaintances that have one they are not using for a night and we will have a grand time of it. I promise you."

He gazed at the girl in front of him and crouched down, looking into her eyes. "Miss de Launcey, are you certain you are all right? You have had a shocking evening, and I must be assured that there is nothing . . . nothing that has upset you too deeply. If it has, say the word and we will leave tomorrow for Shadow Manor."

Andromeda watched her brother, her heart warmed by his seriousness and evident remorse over his inattention.

"I was frightened at first," she admitted. "But then, sir, you should have seen your sister! She punched the fellow in the stomach—I think it was his stomach—and then when he started yelling . . ." She flushed pink, but then frowned and went on. "When he started yelling, she beat him with her umbrella. It was *grand!*"

"Maybe we should put *you* in the ring," he said, chuckling, with a glance over at his sister, who still sat on a hard chair, her hands knotted in an anxious twist on her lap.

"But we would not have had to go through any of that if Miss Neville had not lied in the first place and promised us a place in her fiancé's box, and then retracted it, saying there were others," Belinda said, her tone dark with resentment. "But there weren't! They had no company. The box was almost empty!"

Andromeda, seeing Colin's confused look, explained the invitation and the hasty retraction. She passed over the misunderstanding as delicately as possible, but his expression darkened. "We do not know the entire story," she finished. "It is possible that some of their company had not come yet, or were detained, or were out walking the hallways. We do not know."

"I think we know," Colin said, his expression somber. "She had a strange fit of generosity and then regretted it, no doubt."

"She seemed so genuinely happy to see us yesterday," Andromeda mused. "I do not want to think she just changed her mind."

"She is not the girl we used to know, Andy," he said, putting one hand over hers and squeezing. He stood and straightened. "Anyway, I shall be a better brother and friend from this night forward," he promised. "And we will see the theater the way we should, in high style. But right now, I think everyone should go to bed. I know I will. I have had an exhausting evening."

"At least you are not bruised," Andromeda said.

"Oh, not in any places that you can see, my dear," he said over his shoulder as he limped toward the door. "Not in any places you can see. I will tell you all about it on the morrow."

Six

Another day and another boring musicale . . . or was this to be a recital? Rachel could not remember. She hadn't slept well and she knew she looked haggard, the dark circles under her eyes attesting to a troubled conscience. But throughout her sleepless night she had not been able to forget the puzzled expression on Andromeda Varen's face when she looked up during that awful disturbance at the theater and saw Rachel, seated in elegance and safety, while she and Belinda were forced to flee the pit.

And Rachel could not forgive herself. Strange, since she had never been given to fits of remorse. But Andromeda Varens was an old and valued friend, even if they had not been close for the last few years, and Belinda! Belinda was now her sister's niece. How could she abandon her like that? She was not accustomed to self blame, and as she reflected on the melee, it took all of her considerable willpower to remain seated calmly, gloved hands folded, feet primly together, fan clasped demurely on her lap.

She should have done something. Yarnell, alarmed by the disturbance, had ushered his fiancée and his mother out of the theater to their carriage, and Rachel had searched the crowd for Belinda and Andromeda, but had not seen them. As a result, she had spent a wretched night worried for them. She should have done something, should have said something to Yarnell . . . but she had dithered in indecisiveness, and had, in the end, done nothing. She knew that if anything had happened they would have heard by morning from Colin, but still—

Lady Yarnell and Lady Beaufort, seated on either side of her, clapped politely at the end of a piano piece that resembled the original only in that the right notes were played. But the pianist had no natural ability, and so it sounded leaden and forced, devoid of spirit as no piece of music should be. Nonetheless, Rachel clapped, too.

Just then a beautiful young lady, blond and slim, wearing a gorgeous georgette afternoon gown in pale pink and rose, drifted over to them. "Why, Lady Yarnell, how nice to see you again! And Lady Beaufort. I have not had the pleasure for several years, I believe."

Rachel gazed at her with interest and waited for an introduction. But although Lady Yarnell murmured a greeting, there was no introduction forthcoming. Very odd. Very rude! The young lady, probably a few years older than Rachel, lingered.

Finally Lady Beaufort, after trying to catch her sister's eye, said to the young woman, "Miss Danvers, it is lovely to see you. May I introduce you to Miss Rachel Neville? She is affianced just recently to my nephew, Yarnell. Miss Neville, may I introduce Miss Millicent Danvers? She is a resident of Barcombe, the village near the Yarnell estate."

Rachel nodded politely to the other lady. "Will you sit with us, Miss Danvers?"

"I would be happy to, Miss Neville. What a lovely gown you are wearing! The blue matches your eyes, almost."

Quite in charity with so good-natured a personage, and, if truth be told, quite willing to have her thoughts distracted from her own failings as a friend and sister, Rachel moved over, making space for Miss Danvers. "I was thinking the same of your gown. Not that it matched your eyes, of course, but that it is lovely."

"Thank you. Shall we agree that we are quite the best dressed young ladies here?"

Rachel broke into laughter, but stifled it as Lady Yarnell sent her a quelling look. A lady did not laugh in public and she knew it, but a polite tinkling titter was allowed, was it not? Weary of being censured by her future mother-in-law, Rachel determined to break free, if only for a few moments.

"Miss Danvers," she murmured, her words masked, she hoped, by the introduction of the next recital piece. "I have heard that this house has the most lovely terraced garden, quite an unusual sight for a London house. Our hostess invited us to view it at our leisure. Would you care to see it with me?"

"I would," the lady said with alacrity.

Rachel avoided Lady Yarnell's eyes as they walked away; she already knew there would be censure in them. If Lady Yarnell had not, for some mysterious reason, seen fit to introduce Miss Danvers to her, then she must not have wanted to encourage the acquaintance, for whatever reasons. In her view, no doubt, Rachel should have respected her unexpressed wishes and snubbed Millicent Danvers. The lady was impossible to fathom at times, even when her purpose was clearly understood, for looking at the young lady accompanying her, Rachel could not imagine any justifiable objection to her, especially since Lady Beaufort had ultimately performed the introduction.

Thinking of Lady Yarnell's odd fits and stiff manners, Rachel wondered how she was to go on once inescapably married. She didn't suppose she had fully realized that when one married a man, one married his family as well. Her original stipulations for a husband had included one stating that he must have no female relatives living at home. That had proved untenable, however, given the number of widowed mothers and spinster sisters, aunts, nieces, female cousins and even *daughters* that eligible men seemed to have. So when Lord Yarnell proposed, it had been a joyous day. He had only a younger brother, who was away at school and was soon to take up orders, and his mother. Lady Yarnell she had met only as a cool, distant, but pleasant enough woman.

Her acceptance had appeared to have changed everything. Even though Yarnell had *kindly* informed her that he had made sure of his mother's approval before proposing—he seemed to think that was a point in his favor, or in favor of the match, anyway—ever since, Lady Yarnell had been trying to correct her. She feared she was going from one uneasy situation, her home life at Haven Court, to another.

But she was not married yet. She would at least make her own friends while still unwed.

There were servants posted at various stations to guide those of the guests who had had enough mediocre music and preferred excellent gardens, and Rachel and Miss Danvers soon found themselves in the warm sunshine—or as much of it as could struggle through the London miasma—walking down a flagstone path toward vast banks of flowering shrubs and crowded flower beds. Rachel sighed and turned her face up to the sun for just one second, before shading it again within her bonnet. Unlike her sister, she did not let her skin brown in the sun. It was unladylike.

"It is preferable outside to in on a day such as today, isn't it?" Miss Danvers said. She closed her eyes and took in a long, heady breath of scent-laden air.

"Oh, yes," Rachel agreed, with enthusiasm. "It has been raining so the last couple of days, but even on those days when there was sun, there always seemed to be engagements. Especially when one is preparing for a wedding."

"So you are marrying Yarnell."

Rachel slid a sidelong glance toward the other lady, wondering at the casual use of his name. "Yes. You must know him well, if you know Lady Yarnell and Lady Beaufort."

"Oh, yes, he and I were children together. Or at least he was great friends with my older brother." Miss Danvers's tone implied a negligible childhood friendship.

But it was, Rachel thought, as she murmured a vague "Really?" an opportunity to learn more about Lord Yarnell from one who was likely to be unbiased and who knew him before he became the stuffy marquess he now appeared to be. A sparrow hopped to a low branch in front of them and she paused to watch.

Miss Danvers bent to smell an early rose. "How lovely! The gardens truly are magnificent."

An elderly couple strolled past them and nodded in greeting. Rachel nodded back, recognizing them as ancient acquaintances of her grandmother's. She glanced at her companion. How to introduce the subject she was most interested in without appearing forward? She was about to speak, when Miss Danvers took the lead.

"Miss Neville, I spy a folly in the corner of the garden. Would you like to explore it?"

"I would," Rachel replied, thinking it gave her time to pursue the subject of Yarnell and his tightly furled nature.

They strolled along a path that became mossy as they wound through a grove of trees and found the entrance to the folly, a pretty conceit meant to appear ancient, though it was likely no more than thirty or so years old. Miss Danvers entered first.

"How lovely the gardens appear from the interior, viewed within the framework of gothic arches," she said.

Rachel followed, trailing her gloved fingers over the craggy surface of the stone. "There is a bench by one of the windows. Would you like to sit for a few minutes?"

"Certainly," Miss Danvers said, taking the lead once again.

Once seated, they were silent for a few moments. A bird chirped and warbled, but then was silenced when a fat gray tomcat prowled past, leaping up onto a low hanging branch and sitting in unblinking watchfulness.

"Are you enjoying the Season, Miss Danvers?" Rachel asked, meaning to lead up to the subject gradually of Lord Yarnell and his background as a child.

"Yes. I like London, even though Barcombe, of course, is my beloved home. You must be eager to learn about your new residence. I don't imagine Lady Yarnell has seen fit to tell you anything."

Was there an edge of bitterness in the young woman's voice, or was that Rachel's imagination? She must be careful not to say anything that could be construed as criticism. "True, Lady Yarnell has told me little, nor has Yarnell said much. I suppose they think I will ask anything that I wish to know."

"True."

Millicent Danvers kept her gaze steady on the tomcat, and Rachel examined her profile, the perfect pert nose and high forehead. It was surprising that she was not married. She was so perfectly lovely and with unaffected, pleasing manners. But then Rachel did not know her well. If London taught one anything, it was not to judge by pleasant manners and an attractive façade. Those attributes could conceal a world of deceit and pettiness.

"Are you here with your family?" Rachel asked, becoming more curious about her companion.

"No, I am staying with friends. A girl I went to school with is married to Sir Alexander Pace, and they have a home here in London. She kindly asked me to stay for the Season."

Rachel frowned. She was trying to elicit more information about Miss Danvers's family, but that did not work out well. "How lovely."

They sat in silence for a while.

Finally, Miss Danvers turned to Rachel and said, "I suppose you must be wondering why Lady Yarnell was unfriendly toward me when I approached your group."

Rachel carefully said, "I assumed it only reflected Lady Yarnell's demeanor, which is rather frosty."

The young lady gave a laugh that did not sound at all happy. "Miss Neville, you are clearly a sweet and kindhearted young lady."

Rachel had never been described thus, but let it go. The big gray tomcat leaped. With a squawk and a flurry of feathers drifting on the breeze, the bird was gone. The cat trotted away with it securely in its teeth, heading into a thick shrub to consume its meal in peace.

"Lady Yarnell does not like me because . . . well, my family is in trade."

"How shocking," Rachel said, her tone dry. If that was the worst thing of which the lady could be accused, it did not bear mentioning.

Miss Danvers turned and gazed at her and a beautiful smile lit her face. "How marvelous to meet someone so unspoiled! And with a delightful sense of humor. I like that."

"I did not think I was being funny," Rachel said, raising her eyebrows and looking into the other girl's green eyes. She was startled to see tears welling. "Miss Danv . . ."

"No, it's all right." She put up one hand and looked off, out the window at the sun-touched garden.

"Did I . . ." Rachel hesitated, ever reluctant to pry into someone's emotions. "Did I say something wrong?"

The other girl shook her head vigorously, and, her tears under control, she gazed at Rachel and sighed deeply. "I am just happy," she said, sounding not at all so. "I am so happy you are . . ." She covered Rachel's hand with her own. "Pleasant. Intelligent. Sweet natured. Good." She sighed once more. "And so very pretty."

Rachel was silent, not knowing how to take such an effusion of compliments, especially since she knew she did not deserve at least two of them. She was often not pleasant and certainly not sweet natured.

"You may well think my words strange, and I know they are bold. But I heard there was to be a push this year to find Yarnell a wife, and knowing his mother was to be involved . . ." She trailed off and shuddered. "I was afraid, for Barcombe's sake and . . . and for Yarnell's, that she would search out a replica of herself, cold, stiff, unnatural. I know I shouldn't speak thus, but I am not on good terms with Lady Yarnell, and she is not much liked in our village. With you there is hope that Yarnell can . . . can become again what he once was."

Intrigued, Rachel said, "What he once was? What do you mean?"

"Let us walk again," Miss Danvers said, leaping up from her seat on the bench. She exited the folly, and Rachel was forced to follow. "Yarnell was not always the stiff, proper, rather formal young man you must have seen on occasion," she continued, striding quickly out of the shadows into the sunshine, where she stopped. She turned her face up, closed her eyes, and took a deep breath.

Rachel trotted after her. "I had thought it was his perpetual demeanor," she said.

"On the contrary," the young lady said, reminiscence thick and sweet in her voice. "Oh, on the contrary." She hugged herself, her long fingers clutching her own shoulders. "Once, Yarnell was a hot-blooded young man, willful, vigorous, intense. *Once* he wrote poetry and spun tales. *Once* he . . . but enough." She gazed at Rachel and let her arms fall to her sides.

"From your words," she continued, "I assume you have only seen the cool façade he now presents to the public. He is and always has been a very private person. It may take time to chisel away that exterior, but once you have . . . oh, once you have, you will find Francis, the young man I knew as a girl." She put her hands on Rachel's shoulders and stared deep into her eyes. "Try!" she said, shaking her. "You must, for both of your sakes. If you know anything of life, you must know that it is not worth living if you only skim across the surface like a pretty sailboat on a pond. Our lives are too short; time is too precious. You must dive below the surface to see the teeming activity of the depths. Francis is full of contradictions, a man of many parts, but you will never see any of that if you don't make the effort." She shook her once more and released her hold. "Make the effort. If you love him, *please* make the effort, or he will freeze entirely and become like his mother."

Seven

Colin, restored to vigor by a good night's sleep, strode the length of the sitting room on the first floor and moved a chair slightly, stood back, stared at it, and moved it another fraction of an inch. Andromeda, reading a newspaper by the window where the light was better—vanity would not allow her to wear glasses unless she absolutely had to—looked up and frowned.

"Why are you so agitated?" she said.

Belinda looked up from her book, a text on horses that her uncle had obtained for her before he left on his wedding visit.

Colin paced away and glanced around the room. "I am not agitated, Andy."

"Yes, you are. And do not call me Andy! You promised, Colin! It is vulgar."

"All right!" He went to the window and glanced out, then paced away and cracked his knuckles.

Andromeda winced and grimaced. She hated that sound and had warned Colin repeatedly, but he never remembered when agitated. Ergo, he was agitated. Why, she wondered. "Are you expecting company?" she asked, rattling the paper as she folded it and laid it on the table. She exchanged a look with Belinda, who was listening to the conversation, her book closed over one finger to mark her place.

"Yes, as a matter of fact I am." It was said with a hint of defiance.

She pursed her lips and watched him, but he would not meet her eyes. "Is this what you meant last night by saying you would tell more on the morrow?"

"Yes. I am expecting . . ."

"Sir Parnell Waterford, sir," the butler said, bowing.

The gentleman himself followed, handing his hat to the servant as if he intended to be a while. Andromeda frowned.

Colin strode forward to greet him, pumping his hand vigorously. Andromeda stared, avidly wanting to examine this phenomenon who could so enrapture her normally sensible and staid sibling. She saw a tall man, his skin bronzed and weathered, his pale eyes blazing like aquamarines in his dark face. He was immaculately dressed, from top coat down to Hessians, and his spare smattering of graying hair was carefully combed under the beaver he had just doffed. He was not a picture of dandyism, in other words, but was carefully presented. Appearance would proclaim him a gentleman, but Andromeda eyed him with suspicion. He was involved in Colin's dreadful enthusiasm, and she was convinced no true gentleman would be so deeply enmeshed in the world of pugilism.

"Sir Parnell, may I make you known to my sister, Miss Andromeda Varens, and our charge, Miss Belinda de Launcey? Andy . . . uh, Sister,

Miss Belinda, this is Sir Parnell Waterford." It was said with reverence.

The man advanced, greeted the child first with a pleasantry, and then lingered over Andromeda's hand, his cheeks suffusing with a dull, brick red under the coppery skin. "Miss Varens, so very pleased to make your acquaintance. Sir Colin had much to say about his beloved sister last evening."

His voice was gentle, deep, cultured, wholly unexpected. Their eyes met for a moment, and Andromeda read something there, an earnestness or gravity to his character that was pleasing in some way she couldn't quite explain. She glanced at her brother and felt the color come into her own cheeks.

Colin, eyeing the two with a hopeful, eager expression, said, "I invited Sir Parnell here this morning because I thought, Andy, that if you knew more about the sport of boxing, you would not be so offended by it."

"I am not exactly offended by it," Andromeda said, giving him a look for the use of her despised nickname again. "I just do not think it a fit occupation for a gentleman!"

"Ah, that is where you are mistaken, Miss Varens," the knight said, taking a seat and looking like he wished he had something to do with his hands. "Many gentlemen box, even those in Lord Byron's circle."

"I, unlike many in Society, would not count Lord Byron and his cohorts among 'gentlemen.' Just look at the scandalous way he treated his wife, and then had to flee the country!"

He raised his gray-flecked eyebrows. "Then you are a rare young lady indeed," he said. "Most of the fair sex thought he was the epitome of style and demeanor, I have been led to believe by my feminine relations. I honor you for your intelligent discrimination."

Brightening at his use of the word 'young' in describing her, Andromeda nevertheless was not one to be taken in so easily. She glanced at Belinda, wondering whether the topic of boxing was quite fit for one so young, though she had to remember the girl was an unusual child and had had adventures others her age had not. She had even seen a boxing match, whereas Andromeda had not. The child had cast aside her book and was leaning forward, listening intently, glancing from face to face.

"Some may think so," Andromeda said, continuing on the topic of Byron. "But I find the fellow's writing ostentatious and his purported manner insidiously immoral. His life does not deserve the stamp of 'gentleman,' though I am well aware the title carries with it no guarantee of good behavior. Rather the opposite, I would think, judging from some of the stories I have heard since coming to London."

"Getting back to boxing," Colin said, impatiently, pacing still, "Sir Parnell taught me much last night, And . . . romeda." He goggled slightly on the name, tripping over his usual shortening of it, only remembering at the last minute his sister's preference.

Andromeda bit her lip. It was rather funny, and she smiled. Belinda was giggling behind her hand.

Sir Parnell blinked and looked from person to person. A smile tugged at the corner of his well-shaped mouth, though he could not have known the joke. "Yes, well, your brother, Miss Varens, had a bad experience in his first attempt at a bout here in London. In Yorkshire, no doubt, one can fight the locals in a barroom, but in London, as in everything else, there is a pugilistic protocol. The bout he engaged in was one not sanctioned by those in the know. Here, we fight by Broughton's Rules of Conduct."

"Broughton?" Andromeda had to ask.

"Yes. Did you know, Miss Varens, that it is believed that there is a pugilist buried in Westminster Abbey?"

"Really?" Belinda asked, eyes shining.

"Really," Sir Parnell said, warming to the child and her eagerness. He went on to tell them all about Jack Broughton, a pugilist of some renown who had died in 1789, but whom Sir Parnell, as a very young child, had had the opportunity to meet once before that man's timely end at the age of eighty-five or eighty-six. A Thames waterman in his youth, Broughton became famous for his boxing prowess and formulated the code that bore his name. He also introduced gloves to the practice ring, making it, he felt, a sport fit even for a gentleman.

Andromeda was not impressed. "Are you saying, sir, that no one is ever hurt boxing?"

He fastened his grave gaze on her and said, "No, Miss Varens, I cannot say that." He straightened in his hard chair and crossed his legs. "But I can say that there are many fewer deaths in the boxing ring, proportionately, when the rules of conduct are followed, than deaths on the hunting field during the hunting season. And *everyone* hunts."

"But at least in hunting they are not squaring off and shooting at each other!"

He chuckled. "No. But they also do not have a gun in the boxing ring. And in a proper bout, not one man is drunk, something that cannot be said on the hunting field, I am afraid."

Andromeda folded her hands together. It was inappropriate, she felt, to speak of drunkenness with a child present, but she let it go. "I am still not convinced that this is a safe sport, or one that should be encouraged. Let the brutish masses fight, but Colin is not a brute."

"No, but he is a damn . . . excuse me. My apologies. Not quite used to a lady present and all that, and the child, too, of course." Sir Parnell's dark hue intensified. "He is a fine fighter, miss, if I may say so, judging by the rounds he went with my fellow last night."

"I don't care," Andromeda said, rising. "I do not approve, and I will not condone it with any appearance of approval. Come, Belinda, we have calls to make today."

Rachel sat in the Haven House drawing room listening to her mother and grandmother verbally spar, a sound so familiar to her that she could have taken either lady's part and prolonged the argument with ease.

"I say we have a perfect right to redo this frightful room, regardless of anything Jane may wish. We are Haven ladies, too." That was Rachel's mother.

"But she is the current viscountess," her mother-in-law, Rachel's grandmother, said. "The London house should reflect her taste, not ours."

They sat opposite each other in hard, straight-backed chairs at a small table by the window. Spread in front of them were fabric samples and pattern books, all used in the debate over whether they should consider going further with the necessary renovations to the dreary, glum Haven House.

"Pshaw," Rachel's mother said. "Jane does not have a care in the world one way or the other. She hates London and likely won't set foot in Haven House again if she has her way. You know she doesn't care, you unpleasant old woman. You are just taking the other side to be contrary."

That was a shot close to the truth, thought Rachel, as she watched her grandmother. The old lady's watery blue eyes, so like Lord Haven's, Rachel's brother's, glittered with enthusiasm. The two women had been verbally jousting for decades, the give and take of their sometimes bitter quarrels ringing through the Yorkshire mansion on every subject. There was nothing upon which they agreed, except that the Haven children were the most brilliant and beautiful of any children anywhere.

Rachel, seated on a brocade settee, calmly picked up her needlework and sewed, listening to the fight. Who would win this time? It could be either. Not that she really cared one way or the other. She would be married and then the Haven London house would not matter to her. She would rarely see it.

She dropped her sewing and looked around the room, suddenly panicked, intent on memorizing every stain on the wallpaper, every wear spot in the carpet. It became dear to her as she knew she was

going to lose it, trading it for the elegant Yarnell
house. She felt sick with anticipation . . . or fear.
Marriage was supposed to mean a measure of freedom for a lady, but she felt like she would be going
from one cell to another, more secure and guar-
anteed to last a lifetime. Yarnell and his mother
together made an indomitable force.

Her conversation with Miss Danvers the day before had been repeating over and over in her
mind. What had the woman meant? What more
was there to Yarnell? He never seemed to be
more than a pleasant, well dressed, perfectly
mannered gentleman. The way the other lady
spoke of him, one would think him a veritable
beau, spouting poetry, reading literature, having
romantic adventures. And it was up to her to
bring that out in him? Ludicrous.

The butler bowed his way into the room, and
handed a tray to Lady Haven.

That woman frowned down at the card presented. "Miss Millicent Danvers? And she is here
in person, not just leaving her card? Rachel, do
you know . . ."

"I know her, Mother. I met her yesterday at the
music recital; she is an acquaintance of Yarnell
and his family. Do have her shown in," she said,
rising and turning to the butler. Their guest was
shown in and introductions were performed.
Rachel's mother and grandmother, their interesting dispute interrupted by company, joined in
the conversation for a while, but soon the elder
Lady Haven, exhausted by the day, retreated and
the younger Lady Haven, pleading an appointment and apologizing for any appearance of
rudeness, disappeared.

"I must apologize if this visit is unexpected," Miss Danvers said, now that they were finally alone. "But my acquaintance in London is not large, and I thought since we are soon to be neighbors . . ."

"Please," Rachel said, waving away her misgivings. She was not sure whether she was happy to see Miss Danvers or not, after the odd emotional outburst of the day before. Miss Danvers had, after her outlandish statements about Yarnell, preceded Rachel into the house, after which all conversation by necessity became general, and so there had been no further explanation. But still, she would be a neighbor and friend in future. It behooved Rachel to keep their relationship cordial. And in truth she was not ill disposed toward the young lady. "Do not feel the need to explain. We are 'at home' and happy to have company."

"Are you . . . are you expecting any others?" Miss Danvers said, glancing toward the door.

"No," Rachel replied, not sure how to interpret the lady's hopeful, fearful glance at the door. "I believe you and I shall be quite uninterrupted." She paused for a moment, but then took a deep breath. She might as well use the time to her advantage. "Tell me about Barcombe, Miss Danvers. I do not think I will see it until after the wedding, you know, and I am so very curious."

"It is, unfortunately, too far for a day trip," Miss Danvers admitted. She sat on the worn brocade settee beside Rachel and played with the strings of her reticule. "Barcombe is home," she said simply, shrugging. "I suppose there is the same proportion of good people and bad, pleasant and unpleasant, but I confess I like no place better."

She talked for a while, creating word pictures

of a tiny village with a pond and green in the center, a row of snug shops, a tidy church and vicarage, and a few fine homes set in the placid countryside. There were lovely country walks and another, larger town within a couple of hours' distance, and there were monthly assemblies through the winter at the community hall that drew all the better families for miles around. It sounded delightful.

But, unbidden, wild Yorkshire and the high fells came to Rachel. All her life the dark majesty of craggy cliffs, heather-covered hillsides, and sparkling, trickling gills had been the background of her days. It had been years since she had roamed them in the free way Pammy had until recently, but they were still always there, behind Haven Court, rising above Lesleydale. She had a sudden, powerful urge to see those hills again and to walk them, climbing to the highest prominence and taking in the valley where Lesleydale lay, snug and pretty. She adored London and the excitement of the season, enjoyed the balls and parties, but there was something to be said for Yorkshire, too.

Miss Danvers's gaze slid to the door again, and Rachel glanced in that direction, wondering what the fascination was. They spoke for a while longer, but finally Miss Danvers rose. "I have overstayed my fifteen minutes, I fear." She put out her gloved hand. "Thank you for this," she said, sighing deeply. "Thank you for . . . for this feeling that there will be someone in the Yarnell household who will be a friend to me."

Rachel stood too, and they shook hands. "Don't thank me. I enjoyed the visit likely more than you. And I, too, am glad I shall have a friend in Barcombe. It is so good to hear about the place that will be my home in so short a while."

"Yes. Your home."

Just then the door swung open.

"Miss Neville, I have made myself at home by asking the butler not to announce me. I suppose that is untoward, but I have a surprise . . ."

It was Lord Yarnell struggling through the door with a large wrapped package, and he stopped what he was saying in mid speech and stared at the young woman, Rachel's visitor.

"Millicent," he gasped.

"Francis," she replied, her voice trembling.

Rachel looked from one to the other. Her fiancé's face was bleached a dead white and a fine sheen of perspiration had broken out on his forehead. "Millicent, I . . . who . . . why are you . . ."

"Yarnell," Miss Danvers said, straightening her backbone and standing tall. Rachel noticed she had quickly reverted to a more proper form of address for her childhood friend. "I was introduced to Miss Neville yesterday by your mother and aunt at the musical afternoon we all attended. And she was kind enough . . . I wanted to talk to her about Barcombe . . ."

Rachel, feeling a tension and not sure of the source, said, "Miss Danvers was kind enough to visit and tell me all about my new home. I know so little."

"I never thought . . . you should have said something, Miss Neville," Yarnell said, stiffly. "I wrote a monograph on the topic of Barcombe; you might like to read it. Fascinating, really, the water drainage, and about the vole population balanced by the viper, and the presence of the common polyporus and sulphur tuft fungi."

"She is going to live there, Francis, not study the flora and fauna." Millicent Danvers's tone was acerbic and she slipped back into her familiar mode of address. "She will be your wife, not a botanist!"

Rachel gazed at her in surprise. Lord Yarnell was one of those naturally intimidating gentlemen who carry with them an aura of stiffness and rectitude. She would never think of addressing him thus—and, again, the lady had used his first name! But then, Miss Danvers had known him since they were children.

Since they were children.

Suspicions born the day before took root. She glanced from one to the other of them. Yarnell put down his burden, leaning it against a chair and seeming to forget about it as he stared at Miss Danvers, his face going from white to quite pink, all the way to the tips of his ears. Her lovely complexion colored, too, roses blooming in her cheeks as she cast her eyes down to the floor, the picture of maidenly confusion.

Oh dear, Rachel thought. *What to make of this?*

Eight

A restless night after two days of turmoil created in Rachel an unusual desire to set things right in her own heart. She had never given much thought before to what effect her actions might have on other people, but seeing the wide-eyed horror on Andromeda's face and fear even on the intrepid Belinda's youthful countenance at the theater had made her aware that what she did had real consequences, and she would not always be the one to pay the price for a thoughtless action. It plagued her mind, and she decided she must try to make up for it.

In the normal course of the day she would never see Andromeda, she decided, and so she must make an effort. She had thought about it long and hard, but there was no way to avoid this; she must make amends or . . . or she risked being thought of as a liar and Colin would hate her for her abysmal treatment of his sister. She might not want to marry Colin or care for him as anything but a friend, but their acquaintance was long and friendly, and she would dislike being on bad terms with his family. It was not just the fear on Andromeda's face, evident even at a distance, that haunted her. It was the disappointment.

That Belinda would carry the tale of Rachel's ill treatment back to her sister, Pamela, and new brother-in-law, Lord Strongwycke, also occurred to her. If there was anything in life she feared, it was being disliked as much as her behavior sometimes warranted.

Her maid at her side, Rachel stepped down from the Haven carriage at the Strongwycke residence, a lovely house in a good part of town, much better than Haven House's location. She gazed up at the gleaming white façade and desperately hoped that Andromeda was there—even though this visit was going to be awkward, she would not put it off—and even more so that Colin should be there and see her better behavior. For she had no doubt that the silence from the Varenses the last few days had a resentful edge. Andromeda could not have failed to tell her brother all about the awful melee at the theater, and that while they suffered the insults of the pit, Miss Rachel Neville was sitting in her comfort up in a box. How else could it be construed, when the box around her was virtually empty, but that Rachel had reneged on her invitation on a whim?

And thus this silence from the Varenses. Haven House had not gone one day previous to that without their notice, a note or a visit, or just a calling card left on occasion. But always something. Even Rachel's mother had remarked just that morning that the Varenses had not visited for two days, and with no other acquaintance in the city, she wondered what they were doing. Grandmother had shot Rachel a look, then, catching the guilt, perhaps, on her face. Later, alone together, she said to her middle grandchild, "If there is anything you should be telling us, perhaps now is the time." Rachel, unable to admit to her grandmother what had occurred, had pled ignorance of any problem between the Haven household and the Varenses and fled the room.

She would mend this trifle, explain it away, and then they could all be comfortable again. How, she was not sure, but depended upon inspiration. She sent her card in with the butler, who then came back and said, "Miss Varens is not at home."

'Not at home' could mean she really was not at home, she was not home to visitors, or she was not home to Miss Neville in particular. Accustomed to feeling comfortable about her manners, at least, having had *them* always lauded as the height of perfection even if she was thought over cool or aloof, for the first time she knew the shame of being snubbed, and rightly so. Or perhaps not. Until she actually saw Miss Varens and could explain away her behavior, she could not be sure.

She hesitated, and then, gazing down the street, she said to the sedate butler, "I have called this morning to beg an interview with Miss Varens on a matter of some urgency. Perhaps the lady will have . . . er, come back in from . . . uh, the garden. Would you be so kind as to ask again if the lady is home?" Humiliating. This was humiliating to virtually *plead* for an interview.

The butler, a faintly supercilious expression on his face, bowed, departed, and when he came back it was to say, "Miss Varens begs you to enter."

In that moment, Rachel remembered all the times she had pled a headache, a stomachache, or a prior engagement when the Varenses came to call at Haven Court in the country, and she was ashamed. It was not pleasant to be snubbed by an old friend, and she would never do it again, she vowed.

Her maid took a seat on a bench in the hall, and Rachel, taking a deep breath, tried for an expression that at once announced contrition, pleasure, and gratitude. She could not but fail, and hoped at least the contrition remained. "Miss Varens, how good of you to admit me!" she said, entering the elegant drawing room and advancing to where Andromeda was standing by a table, laying her gloves upon the polished surface.

The older woman cast one quick glance toward the doors that led off to another room, and Rachel wondered if Colin had been there, but would not see her. She quashed a quick resentment. She was trying to do the right thing, if only they would cooperate.

She put out her hand and the other woman took it, a calm, neutral expression on her gaunt face.

Rachel took a deep breath as they both sat on hard chairs near the empty hearth. "I . . . it is a lovely day, is it not?"

"It is," Andromeda said, sitting only on the edge of her seat, as if ready to retreat from the room any moment. "But I do not think you came to discuss the weather, Miss Neville." She glanced toward the partly open door again. "I believe Larkson said you had something of importance?"

Had she ever apologized in her whole life for anything, Rachel wondered. If she had, she would likely be better at this moment. She looked down at her gloved hands, unconsciously noting a loose thread and a wear spot on the index finger. She would have to bring it to her maid's attention. "I was so unhappy to see you at the theater the other night, and know you must have been in the middle of that frightening riot," she began, not sure where to go from there.

Andromeda took a deep breath in, and let it out slowly. Her shoulders sagged. "Yes. I am afraid I misjudged badly the prudence of taking a thirteen-year-old girl to the theater when only pit seating was still available. But I had promised the theater, and I *never* break my word."

Rachel met her eyes then, and knew she had a choice to make. A social lie would suffice. She could say that Lady Yarnell had others coming to the box who were late, or that the others had just stepped out. Or she could say the other party had canceled at the last moment. It trembled on the tip of her tongue. It would hurt no one and would smooth over the incident. The other woman was waiting, and there was a question in her eyes.

But at that pivotal moment an incident came back to Rachel, a scene from her childhood. She was seven and Andromeda was a grand fifteen, a full grown woman to the little girl. Rachel was staying at the Varens estate because there was fever at Haven Court, and little Pamela was ill. One day, bored and at loose ends, she had taken a perfume bottle from Andromeda's dressing table, had spilt most of the contents on the rug, and then lied about it. Though the perfume was clearly important to Andromeda, costly and treasured, she had taken Rachel aside and said to her, in a very kind tone, *Rachel, if you did spill the perfume—and I am not saying you did, mind—and are afraid of the consequences, know this: I will be a little upset that you were playing with my toiletries, but it*

is more important to me that you are honest. I can for-
give anything if you are just honest.

But she had steadfastly lied, and would never
forget the doubt and hurt on Andromeda's face.

She took a deep breath, looked down at her
gloves, but then met the other woman's steady
gaze. "I lied to you when I said that Lady Yarnell
had filled the box that night. In truth . . ." Rachel
glanced away; how to say this next? "My future
mother-in-law is a very prideful and—I will be
blunt, because you are an old friend whom I
trust—unpleasant woman. She is haughty. She
said . . . some disagreeable things about you, and
I knew that if you were in the box with just myself, Yarnell, and his mother, you would be
subjected to her spite." It was not quite the truth,
but this would save Andromeda's feelings best.

Or would it? Was she just saving *herself* again?
Was she still that seven-year-old girl afraid to tell
the truth? She took a deep breath, and continued.
"I would not have you and Miss de Launcey insulted, especially by a woman such as Lady Yarnell.
But also . . . I was thinking of myself, too. I would
be completely honest with you, Miss Varens." She
twisted her hands together and pulled at her
gloves. "Lady Yarnell could make my life difficult
in future if I do not follow her lead and freeze out
those of whom she does not approve."

Andromeda's frozen expression thawed, and
she said, "She did appear to me to be a haughty
and unpleasant woman. You were in a difficult
position." She put out one ungloved, knobby
hand and patted Rachel's. "I knew it had to be
something that would not reflect so poorly on

you as it would if you had just changed your mind on a whim! And I told Colin as much."

Relieved by the other woman's kindness, Rachel yet realized that she had not told the entire truth. If she was honest, she would have to say that she had never once thought of Andromeda and Belinda's feelings in the matter; it had been expediency on her part only. But she vowed to herself never to be so casually cruel again, and never to be so swayed by her own needs. After all, who, in London, aside from her own family, could she trust more than Andromeda and Colin? Who would be kind to her even if all others turned their backs?

"Thank you," she said, humbly, letting out a breath she had not been aware she was holding, "for your belief in me. I do not deserve it."

"Consider the matter over, my dear. After all, though we did not have a box seat with you, ultimately it was my foolish decision to purchase a seat in the pits that put us at risk. I bear the responsibility."

At that moment Belinda came into the room, and her tentative smile said that she had heard what had just passed between the two ladies.

"What say," Andromeda suggested, "we all go to the park, and then for ices?"

And to her surprise, Rachel found that she wanted very much to accompany them. It was a jolly party that set out for an afternoon's adventure.

Evening came, though, and there was a party that Rachel must attend with the Yarnell family group. Now that she was his fiancée, he was taking great pains to introduce her to all of his vast acquaintance. It was dull and somber and respectable, and she was tired after her long ramble with Andromeda and Belinda that afternoon. They had explored corners of London Rachel had never before seen, and had even watched a thrilling military display.

She smiled in reminiscence and Lord Yarnell, sitting beside her as the musicians started their next piece, said, "I would have you not display your feelings quite so openly, Miss Neville. Mother does not consider it good breeding."

Stifling her first response—that she did not care what Lady Yarnell liked or did not like—Rachel remained silent as she examined her fiancé. He was a good enough looking man. Many called him handsome. His perpetual demeanor was cool, courtly, polite . . . but rarely did one see any flashes of genuine feeling on his face. Now she knew that was considered correct in his family.

And yet—

And yet just the day before she had seen the look on his face when he had unexpectedly come across Miss Danvers in the Haven House drawing room. Had there been a preference there at one time? Was there an old romance between them? She could not believe it, considering Yarnell's oft voiced objection to social interaction with the trade class, and Miss Danvers's open acknowledgment that her family was in that sphere.

But there was that look. He had been stunned and discomfited. The few minutes following that confrontation had been excruciating, but Miss Danvers had hurried away, babbling almost in-

comprehensibly about another appointment.
Odd behavior, considering how self-possessed the
young lady seemed. Yarnell had hurried away,
too, after promising to send his carriage for
Rachel the next evening.

She had opened the large package he had left
for her. It was a painting of himself and his
mother, she standing behind his chair with her
hand possessively on his shoulder. Exceedingly
grim, it was, and evoking unfortunate prescience
about the future.

"My lord," she said, touching Yarnell's arm.

"Yes, Miss Neville?"

"May we walk in the conservatory? I have heard
that there are some very fine orchid specimens to
be seen here."

"Your wish is my command, Miss Neville." He
was ever kind, courtly, and cool.

Just once she wished he would display some uncomfortable emotion with her, as he had at the
sight of Miss Danvers.

He guided her toward the conservatory and they
strolled. He kept her decorously to the pathways
where other couples walked; she wondered how to
ask him about Miss Danvers. And what did she really want to know? There were no illusions on her
part that theirs was any great love match. She and
he were marrying because they suited. She wished
for a title, wealth, and a comfortable home. He
married her because . . . why? Why her? There
were a hundred girls with a better dowry and
higher social position. And Yarnell was an acknowledged catch; he could have had his pick.

"My lord, we have known each other for more
than two months now."

"Yes. It has certainly been the happiest two months of my life, Miss Neville."

She slanted a glance toward him to see if he was being facetious, but no, he was entirely serious. She sighed. How could she think otherwise? He was *always* entirely serious. "Thank you. Shall we live in Barcombe most of the year?"

"We have spoken of this already," he said. "We shall come to London for the Season."

"All of us?"

"All?"

"Your mother as well."

"Of course," he said, frowning down at her.

The earthy scent of the potted plants smelled enticingly like spring in Yorkshire. She wondered if she had made a horrible mistake in agreeing to this engagement. Marriage was a necessity, to be sure, but even as a husband, he seemed more likely to side with his mother in any future brangle than with her. Who would be on *her* side at her new home? She could foresee trouble, and did not know how to forestall it.

"Then at least I think we should have our wedding trip to ourselves," she said, testing the waters.

"I thought it would be a good time for you to get to know Mother," he said, with a disapproving tone.

"I would rather get to know you!" she said, stopping suddenly on the path between the tables and turning to look up at him. She studied the expressionless, cool gray eyes and handsome countenance for a trace of warmth.

"We will have our whole lives to get to know each other," he said. "I can't tell Mother no now. She is looking forward to our journey to Wight."

Rachel thought over the examples of new marriages she had seen over the last few months. Her brother, Haven, and new sister-in-law, Jane, were almost indecently mad over each other. It had been embarrassing to see the naked longing in their eyes every time they gazed at each other, until they finally, *scandalously*, ran away to Yorkshire to be married, promising to come back for her wedding.

Even Pamela and her husband, Lord Strongwycke, had both had that intimate expression of secret delight in their eyes. No one who saw them could mistake it for anything but a love match. Rachel had disdained such open and indiscreet demonstration of emotion. She was quite sure that she did not want or need some man desiring her so obviously, needing her so evidently, *wanting* her so very desperately. The thought had frightened her. Wanting her meant he would depend upon her, that she could make him happy or unhappy, and she did not want that emotional entanglement. Yarnell had been perfect, she had opined, because he was as cool and aloof as she was, and would make no embarrassing displays in public.

But surely . . . he was a man. Should he not want to at least kiss her before their marriage? At least once? He had not even when he proposed.

"Yarnell," she said, pulling him toward a private alcove. "Yarnell, would you like . . . that is, I would not object to a kiss, now that we are betrothed."

He recoiled. "Miss Neville, please! You seem . . . different tonight. Perhaps you are unwell. Let us go back to the ballroom and rejoin Mother."

Nine

Clearly agitated, Lord Yarnell escorted her back to his mother and aunt and excused himself. She sat down and tidied her skirts around her, not sure what had just transpired. Was she repulsive to him? Why did he run from her as if she had asked him to do something repellent?

Frowning and biting her lip, not caring if she was mindful of her expression or not for once, Rachel watched Yarnell wend his way through the crowd until he stopped, suddenly, his rigid posture indicating something had alarmed or upset him. Rachel glanced around him and saw the elegant, lovely Miss Millicent Danvers. Like a pantomime, she could see the young lady ask him something, perhaps how he was. He stiffly answered, bowing from the waist in a formal greeting. She reached out one hand in mute appeal. He shook his head and gestured back, toward his family group. She nodded in understanding and was about to turn away, head down.

And then . . . and then he stepped toward her and touched her shoulder.

Rachel watched, spellbound. That one gesture was more natural and spoke more of true caring than every fine word he had ever said to *her.*

Yarnell spoke to her, urgently, rapidly. She drew away and shook her head, but lingered, his hand still clutching her shoulder. He spoke again and finally she nodded, and together they walked across the corner of the dance floor toward the terrace doors and out into the night.

Rachel took in a deep, shuddering breath. She would face it and know it. Her fiancé was in love with another woman. And the woman he loved would not disappear after their marriage. She was a permanent fixture of the village of Barcombe. They would visit back and forth, would see each other at assemblies. She and Miss Danvers would become friends, perhaps.

Was she jealous?

Not really. The music ebbed and flowed around her as she pondered this new knowledge. Yarnell did appear to have hidden depths to him, as Miss Danvers had stated. It was possible that in time Miss Danvers would marry and move away, and she and Yarnell could learn to care for each other. Or the young lady could stay in the village and finally, if she loved him so very much, tempt him into an illicit affair. Rachel did not know her well enough to know if that was possible or unthinkable, morally.

Either way, it would impact *her* life very little. She did not expect to see that much of Yarnell after the first obligatory wedding trip togetherness, and even then, there was his mother. He would have estate business and friends, hunting and gaming and Parliament. If he had a mistress, she supposed she would be relieved, ultimately. She would, perhaps, have her own circle of friends, and pastimes . . . and children.

She frowned and stared off at the hazy view of swirling masses of dancers twisting and twirling in the elegant steps of the waltz.

What would happen if—

No. She could not do that, could not boldly change the course of her life in that manner. It was settled now. Her future was mapped. She moved impatiently on her chair, happy that Lady Yarnell and Lady Beaufort were occupied with acquaintances who sat with them, gossiping in low tones.

But what if she did, Rachel wondered. What if she took a step that would force the issue? What if she confronted Yarnell, told him she knew how he and Miss Danvers both felt, and said she could not marry him under those circumstances?

Insanity! It was insane to even think it. She would put that thought away from her. She had arranged an advantageous match for herself and she would not just give away the dream of her life for the look in two people's eyes.

A young man approached her and bowed.

"Miss Neville," he said. "I am Dexter, Miss Pamela's friend?"

She nodded and greeted him, giving him her hand, though it was not strictly necessary in response to a meeting at a ball.

"Would you do me the honor of standing up with me, Miss Neville?" he asked, nervously. "I would like to ask how Miss Pamela . . . uh, Lady Strongwycke goes on, and Miss Belinda," he added hurriedly, as if she might refuse otherwise.

So it had come to this. She was not sought for her own hand, but as a conduit of information. "Certainly, Mr. Dexter," she said, standing and excusing herself from Lady Yarnell and Lady Beaufort.

As she strolled toward the dance floor on Mr. Dexter's arm, her gaze *would* stray toward the terrace doors. She remembered the look in Yarnell and Miss Danvers's eyes as they met in her drawing room. What *was* there between them, in truth? She must think, and where better than on the dance floor?

June days passed one by one, and Colin felt more confident with each passing day. Every afternoon found him in Sir Parnell's London rooms, gloves on, even as he devoted evenings to his sister and their charge, Belinda.

"You are indeed very good, lad," Sir Parnell said, critically, watching Colin spar with the knight's manservant, more boxer than valet, to be sure, from the looks of him.

"Your tutelage has made all the difference, sir," Colin said, panting and resting his gloved fists on his knees as he bent over to catch his breath.

"Take a break, Roger," Sir Parnell said to the other man, and that fellow grunted and limped away, the worse for wear after a vigorous bout with the young baronet. "Rather, I think we are done for the day. Go get a plaster for that cut on your chin." The fellow left the room.

"I feel for that fellow, sir," Colin said, straightening and watching Roger go, then turning his gaze back to his tutor. "His eye is not good, and I am sure that must affect his reaction. He cannot see as well as I."

"But on the other hand, he has years more experience than you, and he is not so old as his rough visage would indicate. He is thirty-five, no more, I assure you."

"Lord, I took him for fifty!"

"No. Rough living takes its toll. But apart from his eye, his health is very good, I assure you. It is just that you have exceeded his skill, and it is showing." Sir Parnell offered Colin a cloth. "In fact, I think you are ready for your first proper bout," he said.

Colin felt a trickle of excitement in his stomach as he mopped the sweat off his face and neck. "Do you really think so?"

"I do. I have never seen a *gentleman* with such natural ability."

"That is damning with faint praise, certainly," Colin said, throwing himself into a chair.

"Not at all. There have been many fine gentleman boxers of late." The knight, his pale eyes shadowed by his brows as he frowned in thought, strolled away. Over his shoulder, he casually said, "Shall you be seeing your sister later today?"

"Yes. We are going to the theater tonight; I have box seats from a fellow I went to school with. He must leave town for some errand on his estate. I have promised Andy to spend some time with her and the child. We have already been to see the Tower and other sights. Tonight is the theater." He did not mention their previous bad experience.

"The theater," Sir Parnell said. "My! I have not been this age."

Colin stopped mopping his brow and watched the older man for a moment. He had only known the man a week, but knew him enough to sense interest. "Would you . . . join us, sir? It will just be a family party."

"Could I?" Waterford said, meeting the baronet's gaze. "I would not be . . . intruding?"

"Not at all."

"You are sure your . . . sister would not disapprove?"

"Not up to her to approve or disapprove," Colin said, carelessly. "My party; I'll invite whom I like."

"But I would not want to upset her. She might not want me there," he said, and there was a wistful tone in his voice that Colin did not understand.

"Why would she not?"

"I don't think she approves of me, and she certainly does not approve of my training you in pugilism."

"As I said, sir, it is not up to her to approve or disapprove you. You are my friend, and I will invite you where I like. She has nothing to say in the matter. She need not come if she does not like you."

Colin saw something like hurt on the knight's weathered face. But the man nodded.

"However," he said, "this theater party is meant for her and the child, am I right? Please ask her permission. I will not come, else."

How strange, Colin thought, as he gathered his coat and hat, preparatory to going home. "I will send you notice once I get home, sir, about the theater tonight," he said, holding out his hand.

"And I will arrange your first bout, Sir Colin. I should be able to tell you more by this evening."

The two men shook hands and parted.

Later, in his bath, Colin leaned back against the copper tub and smoked a cigar, pondering on all the changes in his life since arriving in London. He was almost ashamed to think back now. He had come to London in a panic, knowing that Rachel was looking for a husband, and hoping to interfere with the process and finally get her to see that he was the best candidate for her hand. From there he had proceeded to blunder into a proposal to her younger sister, Pamela, confusing that poor girl, who had always, apparently, liked him and thought him husband material. He hadn't known that until a frank discussion with Haven, his old friend and neighbor. All it had done was confuse Pammy hopelessly, when she had a proposal already from the man who was now her husband and the love of her life, the Earl of Strongwycke.

I have blundered around like a bloody bull in the market square, he thought, sending a smoke ring up to the ceiling. A maid entered and poured more hot water into his bath, and he closed his eyes, relaxing in the luxurious, herb-scented water. The Strongwycke household was run on sumptuous lines and he had set himself to enjoy it while it was available. It was not that the Varens estate was austere, but there was a definite difference between an earl's household and a baronet's.

He pondered his future. Marriage was not for him, perhaps, though he would like to be married. He would like children, and he would like a woman who would be there at the end of the day to talk to, to be with, to make love to.

Rachel. He tried to dismiss her picture from his mind. She was only there because he had gotten used to thinking of her as his future wife, that was all. He would now erase her—

Though she had looked so splendid the last time he saw her. And even as angry as he had been with her over the theater episode, he still had never seen or met her equal. And she had humbled herself enough to apologize to Andy, and very handsomely, too, his sister had said. There was a warmth there now when he thought of her.

It was not love, though, he reminded himself. It was just friendship. That was all there would ever be between them, that friendship.

And yet—the warm water swirled around his loins and he felt the old, slow arousal, the stirring as he thought of her, imagined kissing her lips, touching her petal-soft skin, caressing her breasts. She was the only woman who had ever moved him that way, made him want her with just a glance, just a touch. He had been with women, but not one could compare to Rachel. Nor ever would, he feared.

A million times he had imagined every detail of their wedding night, down to the moment when he claimed her as his own, his love forever, and then, after, gently showed her what pleasure could be between a man and a woman. And yet she was so cool. Did he know for sure that a fire burned within her somewhere? Every shred of evidence said no, that she was cold through and through. But instinct told him, whispered that she was afraid, that she was deeply passionate and that was why she hid it so well, tamping it down and freezing it out.

The maid came back in with a large, soft towel, and he stood up from his bath. Her cheeks turned bright pink as she offered him the wrap, and he was puzzled until he noted the state his thoughts of Rachel had brought him to, and where the maid's eyes had wandered. He felt his cheeks turn ruddy and he wrapped himself quickly.

"Send my valet in, will you, Anna?"

She ducked her head and bustled out, and he heard her giggling in the hallway with another maid.

He dried himself, pulled on a robe, and moved toward the fire. He must quell his sensual thoughts, especially since he knew there was no way he would ever achieve the object of his desire, Miss Rachel Neville. He must not delude himself that there was some hidden ember within her that he could coax into a flame. She was beyond his touch forever, and would soon be married to that fubsy-faced, frosty iceberg, Yarnell.

He felt the surge of anger in his veins, the fire that burned whenever he thought of the marquess and how he would soon own the fair Rachel, body and soul. He breathed deeply, quelling it, unballing his fists, consciously relaxing his taut stomach muscles. "Save it for the ring, boy," he said to himself, his voice echoing oddly in the master bedchamber. "Save it for the ring."

Ten

"What is your problem, girl?"

Rachel looked up as her grandmother entered the drawing room, leaning heavily on her cane but carrying a roll of fabric under one arm and trailed by a footman with more bolts of material. "There is nothing wrong with me, Grandmother." She tossed aside her sewing. She hadn't laid a stitch in it for an hour anyway.

"There is," the woman asserted, her voice querulous. "You're sickening for something. What is it?"

"I miss Pammy. And Haven. Our family is breaking up."

"And soon you will be wed to that long-toothed sober-side and gone, too." She hobbled farther into the room. "Aren't you looking forward to it? It is all you have talked of since you were fourteen."

Primly, Rachel said, "I am indeed looking forward to marriage, and to being Lady Yarnell."

The dowager stared at her for a minute, then waved the footman to deposit his burden and be gone. She added her own roll of fabric to the pile and, tapping over to her middle grandchild, she sat down in a chair near her with a groan. She had lived for more than eighty years, and had not been especially dull of wit even as a child. With the added experience and observation of all those years, she was considerably sharper than many people thought.

She leaned forward, supported by her cane, and gazed into Rachel's face. Many had said that her gaze pierced through the shell of protection most people threw up around their soul. What a bunch of rubbishy nonsense! She just chose to see people's actions and interpret them. Few folks were truly impenetrable. Rachel, though, was often one of those few. She maintained the façade of an elegant lady even when she was deeply disturbed.

But there was something wrong, and as badly as she and Rachel got along, she loved her grand-daughter fiercely and hated seeing her unhappy. And the girl *was* unhappy. "You, child, are a liar." She straightened from her examination.

"Oh, Grand!"

"Hmph, you never call me that. What's got your tail in a twist?"

Rachel stood and paced the length of the room to the fireplace and stared up at the baroque hearth, the twisted gargoyles and fanciful birds. She put out one hand, blindly it seemed, and touched a tendril of carved ivy leaves. "There is nothing wrong. I have exactly what I want in life, what I have been looking for. Lord Yarnell is a good man, and wealthy beyond even my dreams. He likes me and wants to marry me."

The dowager felt her stomach wring as if some-one with strong hands was twisting it in their grip. There was so much unhappiness in the child's voice, all the more desperate because she was trying so hard to suppress it. That she was so easy to read was a testament to how deeply disturbed the girl was. The dowager had never truly understood Rachel, because the child was so self-contained and aloof. Since she was thirteen, shortly after her father died, actually, she had retreated into a shell and stayed there.

But she had always seemed happy enough in a calm, self-possessed way. There were no wild ups and downs the way her sister, Pamela, experienced them. Everyone—including her grandmother—had always assumed she just did not feel things very deeply.

Could they have been wrong?

"Child, come here."

Rachel was reluctant—it was there in the stiff line of her backbone, the rigid set of her shoulders—but she obeyed.

"Sit!" As Rachel sat before her, the dowager set aside her cane and took the girl's face within her two bony, knobby hands and stared into her pale, lustrous eyes. She looked deep, reading, learning, and was startled to see two giant teardrops squeezing up into the corners of her eyes.

"You have a grave decision to make and do not know what to do, is that true?"

Rachel gasped, and brushed away the tears as her grandmother released her face. "How did you . . . what do you mean, Grandmother?"

The dowager shook her head, slowly, not even sure how she knew what she knew. "You have always been the child I did not worry about. You seemed to know what you wanted from the day you were fourteen, and so I believed you, believed you could handle things on your own without my elderly interference. But now I see turmoil in your eyes, indecision. You do not know what to do about something, and I must imagine it has something to do with your marriage."

Rachel collapsed on the table in front of her, burying her face in her arms and sobbing. The dowager stroked her head, letting her get it all out, winding the chestnut curls around her knobby arthritic fingers and feeling love for her middle grandchild swell into her heart and fill it, like springwater in a newly drilled well. The girl had not cried since . . . since the night her father had died.

But a lack of tears did not mean a lack of feeling.

"My son loved you best of all his children. Did you know that?" she asked Rachel.

Rachel nodded, even though her face was still covered and the tears were still flowing.

"It hurt you badly when he died, did it not?"

She nodded again. "He w-was the only one who ever loved me," she sobbed.

"Nonsense. I love you. And your mother! She thinks the world of you, too, child!"

"Mother loves me as long as I do well, like now, with Yarnell. But if . . . if I was not to make this brilliant match . . ." She shook her head, raised her face, and sniffed back her tears. "Mother really loves Haven best; we all know it. He is her golden boy, even when she is berating him."

The dowager cocked her head on one side. "I have not thought that, but perhaps you are right. That's not important right now, though; you are. Let us come to the present day. You aren't sure about Yarnell, is that it?"

Rachel shook her head slowly. "I . . . don't know. I *was*. He truly is a good man, Grandmother, I know he is. He is a little haughty; I know that. But I have been accused of that, too. That is why I thought we would suit; I understand him."

The dowager sat back and listened, amazed at the self-knowledge the girl had when she had always thought Rachel single-minded and indifferent to others' opinions. "You were, as a child, the sweetest of all the children, the most vulnerable, I always thought. Haven, being a boy, had a natural toughness to him and Pamela was resilient, like a willow, bendable, but you . . . I have never seen anyone hurt so deeply as you, when your father died."

Rachel was silent for a long minute, and her voice, when she did speak, was broken and quiet, clogged with tears. "I knew when he died that no one ever again would love me so deeply, without reservation, without hesitation. And I knew I would miss that."

The dowager watched Rachel as she wiped the tears from her eyes in an uncharacteristically inelegant movement, and remembered Sir Colin Varens and his oft-repeated proposal. She had always ridiculed the fellow for his devotion to Rachel in the face of Rachel's unwavering rejection of his suit. Did the boy know something they had all missed? Was Rachel really the passionate, tenderhearted one in the family, and had she submerged that side of herself out of fear of pain?

"What is it now that gives you doubt about your marriage?" she asked, wanting to get to the heart of the problem. Who knew how long this strange fit of openness would last before Rachel would shut again as tightly as a clam? She laid her knobby hands flat on the table in front of her, then scratched at a groove in the wood with one thick fingernail.

"I am afraid he loves someone else."

She stopped her scratching.

"What?" Whatever she had expected, it was not this. "What do you mean?"

Rachel told her the tale of meeting Miss Millicent Danvers, and seeing her fiancé's reaction to the young lady. She seemed not so much jealous as puzzled.

"If there is feeling between them, why are they not betrothed?"

Rachel nodded, as if her grandmother had hit what she herself had been wondering. "Well, Miss Danvers's background is in trade. Yarnell is . . ."

"A long-nosed, sour-faced elitist."

"Grandmother, I am only guessing about the . . . the division between them. There could be other reasons, more personal things."

"And you are guessing at the love, too, are you not?"

"Yes. I have no proof. Just the way they look at each other."

"Do you love him?"

"No. No, I don't."

"Are you still intent on marrying him?"

Rachel sighed. She covered her face with both slim hands. "I don't know! I just do not know." She uncovered her face and shrugged. "I don't know."

The dowager decided to approach the problem from the opposite end. "Why does it matter to you if he is in love with another woman?"

Wistfully, Rachel gazed off out the dirt-clouded

window. Her gaze was unfocused. "Lately, it seems as if everyone is in love . . . with someone. And they all look so happy."

This was a new side to her grandchild, one that she had never seen, and the dowager did not quite know what to say, except, "Ask him. You must ask him if he is in love with the Danvers chit. You will not be happy until you know the truth."

"I can't do that, Grandmother. And our wedding has already been announced. I think I am better off not knowing." She sighed again. She straightened her back and stiffened, taking in a deep breath and letting it out slowly. "No, our future is set. Yarnell and I will marry and be happy. He is a good man, and I can be his wife and raise our family."

The dowager frowned as she watched the coolness set in, like frost on an October night stealing over her. Rachel's slim fingers checked her hair, making sure no stray curls escaped her perfect style, and she adjusted her lovely dress, settling the folds into perfect order. The dowager liked the other Rachel much better, the one who was uncertain and misty. But this was the one she was accustomed to. Finally, she said, "You must do what you think best, Rachel, but remember; you only have one life. Live with no regrets."

Live with no regrets. Her grandmother's words echoed unexpectedly in her head, taunting her with the temptation of life lived on terms other than society's rigid expectations. What would she do if she had only herself to consult, only her own pleasure and desires, and not societal strictures? Rachel pondered that for the rest of the day.

"Lord Yarnell has arrived, Miss Neville." The butler bowed in her fiancé, who looked as dapper and neat as always.

"Miss Neville, you look blooming," he said, coming forward and kissing her hand.

"Yarnell," she said, coolly.

"I thought we would go for a drive in the park. Would you like that?"

His uncertainty was endearing, in a way, and Rachel saw a flash of what Miss Danvers was perhaps speaking of when she had mentioned his charm. "I would like that," she said, smiling up at him.

She called her maid and donned her bonnet and pelisse, and took his arm as they exited.

"I brought the landau. We will have . . . Miss Neville?" He looked back up the steps at her.

Rachel had stopped at the top of the steps down to the street. There, in the landau, was Lady Yarnell, sitting grimly and waiting for her son and his future wife to join her.

"I did not know your mother was to accompany us," Rachel said, in a strangled tone. "I thought we could talk."

"We can talk," he said, looking up at her with a frown. "Miss Neville, you can say anything in front of my mother. She is to be your mother soon, too, you know." He stepped up the two steps to where she stood, frozen, took her hand, and led her to the carriage.

The ride to the park was accomplished in grim silence. The landau was elegant but ponderous, and the park was crowded. Yarnell, Rachel had noticed, was always more silent and reserved in his mother's presence, and since she was usually around, he was generally silent.

They passed a carriage of older people at one point, and Lady Yarnell said, "Yarnell, have Coachman slow. I wish to talk to Mrs. Forest for one moment."

The carriage was duly stopped, and Lady Yarnell leaned over the edge and talked to her acquaintance.

"Yarnell," Rachel said, in a low tone. "I must speak to you."

"About what, Miss Neville?"

He kept a decorous six inches between them at all times, but Rachel moved closer and hissed, "Not here. Will you walk with me?"

"I don't think . . ."

Rachel summoned all of her considerable firmness, and said, "I will go no farther until we talk, Yarnell. Let us stroll, and meet your mother farther along."

Disconcerted and frowning, Yarnell acquiesced, though Lady Yarnell was still asking what they wanted to walk for, what they were to talk about, and why they needed to leave her alone, as they walked away.

Once alone, Yarnell said, "Miss Neville, I am not accustomed to being rude to my mother. What is this all about, and why must we walk when we have a carriage?"

Her lips clamped together, Rachel guided him to a quiet, tree-lined walk and stopped, turning and gazing up at him. A breeze riffled through the trees, but she noted it did not dare lift his thick hair, so well had it been damped down and

rigidly styled. "Yarnell, first, I think as your fiancée I deserve as much consideration as your
mother, and I would think you would wish to be
alone with me on occasion. That you do not does
not show a proper amount of feeling toward the
woman who will be your wife and bear your children." As she talked, she felt a freedom taking
wing in her heart. She had been silent too long,
and it was not like her.

"Miss Neville, I must say this outburst is most
unlike you, and it borders on . . . on insolence. I
do not like this loose talk of children, and I dislike very much that you felt compelled to drag
me away from my mother. It shows an improper
lack of feeling." His voice was hideously priggish
and his expression was prim.

Anger welled up into her heart. "I will not be
treated as second best to your mother, Yarnell. So
if you chose me as a wife because you thought I
would be silent and scared, then I am the wrong
wife for you." She took a deep breath. "But that
is not what I drew you aside to talk about, although it is high on my list of things we need to
straighten out. Foremost on that list is something
entirely different. My lord, are you in love with
Miss Millicent Danvers?"

Eleven

She had not thought he would answer, but he did, and without hesitation.

"Yes, I do love Miss Danvers. But I do not see what that has to do with us."

She was stunned, so stunned that she could not think or talk. Of all the things she had expected him to say, yes was not one of them. She had expected to have to worm it out of him or coax it or possibly never know the whole truth. But he said it so boldly, as if it was a small matter, and not worth speaking of.

"You . . . love her?"

"I do. Our love is old, existing since we were children."

"Ah, you love her as a friend, then!" There was some relief there.

"No." His expression was serious, thoughtful. "I love her as . . . as a woman." He clasped his hands behind his back and looked down at the ground. "I will always love Miss Danvers. She will ever be first in my heart."

Hearing herself speak with a detached tone, Rachel said, "And yet you saw fit to affiance yourself to me?" The day had taken on an unreal quality. Who would have thought she would be forcing a confession out of her fiancé that he loved another woman? They were to be wed in just six months!

"I do not see what one has to do with the other, Miss Neville." His tone was cool, but he would not meet her eyes. He gazed now over the green lawn toward a group of gentlemen and ladies strolling down a pathway. "Millicent is not suitable to be the wife of a marquess, unfortunately. I would wish things were different, but they are not." He took a deep breath and stiffened his back. "I am a realist. You are perfectly suitable. You are beautiful, so I may hope any children we are so fortunate to have will be physically well looking, though that is not of primary importance to me. Your family is old and honorable and of good character, even if your grandmother is so very odd. But she will not live long and we will seldom be near Yorkshire, so that does not signify. And you yourself have the demeanor and stance of a true lady, well behaved, elegant. My mother approves of you; that was a primary consideration for me. And you have no unfortunate connections to trade."

He enumerated all those things so easily. He must have thought it out thoroughly. Rachel would have liked it better if it were not so. It sounded so cold recounted like that, and yet had she not chosen him on exactly those grounds? She had had a list of requirements, and he fulfilled more than any other gentleman who had expressed an interest in her. It was that simple. It was that cold.

She stumbled away from him toward the tree. She reached out blindly and felt the bark under her gloved hands. Everything at a distance, even the feel of nature must be barricaded with silk. She stripped off her glove and laid her hand against the rough texture, feeling, as if for the first time, minute traces of moss, the ancient trails of insects, and the sharp edge where some bark had just broken away.

All her life since she was thirteen she had been keeping things—people, emotions, pain—at a distance, as though sensing it only through silk. Edges blurred, sensation muted.

Yarnell offered her a life lived that way. He would never intrude on her pain, never expect more from her than courtesy. Day would follow day and there would be no turbulence, no untidy emotions to contend with.

Perfectly civil, perfectly calm, perfectly cold. Life viewed through a smoky glass, all of the sharpness blurred and bearable.

"Miss Neville," he said, gently. "I have, perhaps, been remiss in answering your questions with such honesty. But I would have that between us, at least."

Rachel nodded absently and stroked the tree trunk, the sharp bark prickling the tender pads of her fingers. Honesty. If only she had been honest with herself before now. A stray beam of sun found her face and touched her lips and cheek, warming her. She closed her eyes and turned her face toward it, feeling the warmth seep into her.

What a fraud she was, telling herself this was what she wanted, making herself almost believe it. The veil had slipped once or twice. She had been on the verge of telling someone, anyone, that she wanted to go home and think for a while, forget about the London Season this once.

She loved London, with all of its bustle and hurry, but it was no place to think.

But now she knew there was one thing she did not need to think about. One thing she must do while she had the courage, while she still could.

"My lord," she said, turning and pulling her tight-fitting glove back on with jerky, hard motions. "I find, after giving the matter much thought, that we shall not suit."

"I have upset you," he said, chagrined. "Miss Neville, I never meant to hurt your feelings. My emotions for Miss Danvers will always, I assure you, be kept in the strictest check. I will never, by thought or deed, betray . . ."

"Then you are a fool," Rachel burst out and strode away from him.

He caught her arm and whirled her around. "What did you say?"

She stared up at him, noting that his dark eyes were blazing with sudden anger, the first real emotion she had seen on his face toward her. "I said you are a fool." She searched his eyes, reading life beneath the surface. What had made him hide from emotion as she had? She would never know. Didn't really care to, if the truth could boldly be said. "You have real, lasting love in the palm of your hand, and yet you reject it? You are an idiot. You are rich. You are powerful. Whomever you marry becomes instantly acceptable, and you must know that. There can be no true objection to Miss Danvers, who is everything genteel and ladylike. If you let your mother keep you from marrying the woman who holds your heart, then I would not marry you ever, for you are *not* a man!"

His expression bespoke fury, first, and then

bafflement. "Are you . . . are you jilting me, Miss Neville?"

"I am, Lord Yarnell. And if you do not, this instant, go to Miss Millicent Danvers, fling yourself at her feet, and *beg* her to marry you, then I think you are the greatest fool I have ever known. If you have an ounce of passion in your heart, you will not let any man or woman keep you two apart."

"I do not think we have anything more to say to each other," he said, in a voice heavy with resentment.

"You are correct."

"I will escort you home."

"Thank you."

With the plans of a lifetime crumbled to dust about her feet, Rachel stayed home that evening for almost the first time since they had come to London nearly three months earlier. She did not tell her mother or her grandmother of her decision, made in haste and repented only for the fuss and bother she would have to endure. There was, she found, great emotion attendant even upon a decision which one felt forced into, even one for which there seemed no alternative. She could not go out and face Society just yet. For all she knew, Lord Yarnell and his mother could make her life very difficult in London if they made it known that she was a jilt, and she might have to retreat to Yorkshire.

But for now, all she wanted was to stay home and think.

Her mother fussed over her for a few minutes when she stated she was staying home, asking if

she was sick, but since it was clear that she was
not ill, eventually the woman left her alone and
went off to a card party.

So she was alone, sitting by the window in the
ugly drawing room.

What would she make of her life? She had fulfilled the plan of her lifetime only to find it did
not suit, so what now? She did not regret her decision to jilt Yarnell and would do the same
again. Let others view it as they may, she had, for
a while, begun to see that life with the marquess
would be dreary and the company of his mother
insupportable. And he would never love her
enough to defy his mother. The only hope for
Yarnell was if he could cut the strings that bound
him and marry Miss Danvers. If he did so he
might become a man. She did not hold out
much hope for that.

She sat for hours, watching the sun set, the sky
muddy with indefinite clouds and smoke from
thousands of coal fires. How did one live life without a plan, she wondered. Did others meander
through life with no clear object? And did life answer with the gift of a purpose?

A footman came in and lit the evening candles,
and Rachel heard the tap-tap-tap of her grandmother's cane on the floor outside the drawing
room door. There was a hesitation, and then the
door opened behind her. She looked over her
shoulder and smiled.

"What are you doing sitting here alone in this
gloom?" the old lady asked. "You sickening for
something?"

"No."

"For the first time, I think that is the truth."

The dowager grunted and sank into a chair with a groan. "I am getting old. I suppose I have known it for some time, but I feel it more this spring."

"At home you do not do so much. You are just tired with all of the visiting and parties."

"True."

Rachel could almost feel her grandmother's perspicacious glance, the question that would likely be writ in the watery blue eyes. She knew she was behaving differently, but did not feel like explaining to anyone yet how her life had changed. There would be time enough for that tomorrow, time enough for decisions and plans. Right now all she wanted to do was sit and watch out the window as carriages took people away for their evening's engagements and brought people for a card party in a town house three doors down.

Life observed at a distance. Hadn't that always been her way? And yet she was poised on the threshold of something. She just didn't know what it was yet.

Her grandmother cleared her throat to speak, but at that moment the butler came into the room and bowed. "A note, Miss Neville, for you."

Rachel took the note and unfolded it.

Miss Neville,

Forgive my presumptuousness in writing this hasty note to you, but I must say thank you. Francis has told me what you said and did. We are on our way this moment to the continent. We will marry at Dover before we go. Thank you. I already said that, did I not? But I will never find adequate words to express how deep my gratitude. My wish

for you is that you find the love you so obviously de-
serve for your selfless, gracious, benevolent heart.
                              Yours,
                              Millicent Danvers.

Rachel smiled and refolded it, glancing up at
her grandmother. With just a moment's hesitation, she handed the note over to the other
woman, who unfolded it and held it close to the
candlelight, adjusting her spectacles, which always hung on a ribbon around her neck.

"Francis . . . that is Yarnell, is it not?" The dowager looked up at Rachel and there was an odd
expression on her face. "Selfless? Benevolent?
What does this mean? This Miss Danvers, is she not
that chit who visited the other day? And the girl
you told me of, the one Yarnell is in love with?"

"Yes." Taking a deep breath, Rachel said, "I
jilted Yarnell. Told him we would not suit."

"And he has eloped with Miss Danvers?"

"Yes. They have an old connection, and he told
me today that he loves her. It was all I could do.
They should not have been kept apart by our engagement."

The old woman gazed at her shrewdly, squinting against the glare of the candle between them.
"Going to play up the martyr angle, are you?
Won't fly with your mother, you know, who will
damn you as a fool. Doesn't play with me, either,
young lady, since I know you better. In many ways
you are more like me than any of my grandchil-
dren. You had already decided you didn't want to
marry him, hadn't you? What would you have
done if there hadn't been a Miss Danvers?"

Rachel first smiled, then felt a bubble of laughter that was irresistible. She chuckled first, then laughed outright, and then threw back her head and guffawed. The dowager joined her, and their laughter echoed in the cavernous, high-ceilinged room.

"I was so relieved," Rachel gasped, wiping tears away from her eyes. "I detest his mother, and he had not the intestinal fortitude to stand up to her. I would always have been second best until the day that wretched woman died, and I would have despised Yarnell for his lack of courage. Mother is nothing to her!"

"And so how did you find out about his feelings for Miss Danvers?"

"I inferred from things she said." Rachel sobered. "She said he was romantic and poetic. She told me things about him that I could not conceive, and I saw it in their faces when they met. So I asked him, and he admitted that he loved her and always would, even though he still fully intended to marry me. I had the opportunity to do something . . ." Rachel stopped on the verge of saying that she had done what she did out of selfless altruism. "No."

She laughed out loud. "No!" she repeated, and it echoed off the ceiling. "I was going to paint myself as the kindhearted lady who wants to see true love triumph, but the truth is, I could not see myself being second or third my whole life, first to his mother and then to the woman he would always love and want. When I told him our engagement was over, I did not even know for sure that he would go to Miss Danvers. In fact, I rather thought he would not, his pride and his feelings of family obligation are so great." She told her grandmother about the objections to Miss Danvers from his family.

"It changes how I view him," the dowager said, "that he would elope with her. I would not have believed it of him, and must say I *will* not until I see the notice in the paper. What will you do now?"

Rachel shrugged. "I don't know. I'm frightened. I have always had a plan, though it often was averted by circumstance. But I always knew I needed just one good Season in London, and I would find my husband and make my mark on Society. I had that opportunity. Yarnell still wanted to marry me, even after admitting to me that he was in love with another woman. And pride would not have stopped me. I had no real reason to believe that if I rejected him he would marry Miss Danvers." Pensively, she added, "Though I am happy for them, especially for her. She loves him so, and she has always been faithful in that love. She would have been a good friend, even if Yarnell and I had married."

The old lady stood and hobbled around to her grandchild. She put one arthritic hand on the younger woman's shoulder, and said, "I am proud that you have done this, for whatever reason. Your mother will not be happy and there may be some difficulty if it becomes known that you jilted Yarnell. But you will prevail. I advise that we stay in London, defy the gossips, and that you enjoy yourself. Just enjoy the Season without a goal, for once."

Rachel thought about it for a minute, covering the old woman's hand with her own, letting her youthful warmth seep into the arthritic joints. "Perhaps you're right, Grandmother."

"Why have you never just called me 'Grand,' like the others?"

Rachel grinned. "It seemed too familiar for so grand a lady as yourself. You require the full title of your name."

The woman cocked her head on one side. "I have misjudged you, my dear. I have sorely undervalued you, and I find myself in the unenviable position of having to apologize. You have more bottom to you than I ever would have thought possible."

"Do I? I'm not so sure. I have been used to thinking well of myself, but I don't know what to think right now."

"You will know if you just let your heart guide you." The dowager shook herself and dropped her hand away from Rachel's shoulder. "I begin to sound like the worst sort of romantic now, and I will leave off before I tell you that true love will find you, for it very well may not, and then wouldn't I look like a maudlin old fool? I am going to bed now, my dear. We will tell your mother in the morning."

Rolling her eyes, Rachel said, "It is the one thing I dread."

"Oh, then let me," the old woman said, her eyes glittering. "It would give me something to look forward to."

"Grandmother, you are an evil old woman."

"I know. And it is something to anticipate in your future, my dear. Plan for it. There are endless opportunities for amusement."

Twelve

Colin, whistling a merry tune, jaunted down the stairs of the Strongwycke mansion, thinking that despite how the Season had started, all in all he was reasonably satisfied with how things were going. He and Andromeda had received a note from Lord and the new Lady Strongwycke. They were at Shadow Manor and blissfully happy, riding every day, making plans, and looking forward to having Belinda back in a month. They had sent a kind letter to her, too, with a package of gifts and books.

Andromeda had her interests, and Belinda went with her everywhere. Sir Parnell was fast proving to be as good a friend as he was a trainer, and had scheduled a bout for Colin in two days. Life was good.

He strode into the morning parlor, where he knew Belinda and his sister would be making their plans for the day, and was startled to find Rachel there, her head bent close to Belinda's over a pattern book of dresses.

Both looked up.

"Hallo, Uncle Colin," Belinda said, in the form of address she had decided on of late. He rather liked it, since he had no nieces or nephews in reality.

"Hello, Colin," Rachel said, her cheeks pink for some unfathomable reason.

Andromeda, seated at a nearby table, glanced from one to the other and said, "We have just been planning our assault on the *ton* tonight. Miss Neville has kindly invited me to a ball given by an acquaintance of hers."

"I have my friend's permission to invite as many guests as I wish," she said. "And since there is always a dearth of . . . of eligible gentlemen, would you come, too, Colin?"

Speechless, he stood and stared. Damn. Just when he thought he had defeated his powerful longing for her, she arrived, looking adorably springlike in pale green and yellow. And she spoke to him in such a manner that his heart thrummed heavily. "I . . . I . . ."

"Do say you will," she urged, prettily.

Her pale eyes, the color of the Yorkshire sky scrubbed clean after a storm, were wide, fringed delectably with brown lashes. He had seen enough of London ladies to know that not a one compared to her in looks or in spirit.

"I don't think . . ."

"Colin," Andromeda said, standing suddenly and laying aside the invitation she had been reading. "May I speak to you? Privately? If you would forgive this out of our old friendship, Miss Neville?"

"Of course, Miss Varens," Rachel said, looking disconcerted and blushing an even deeper shade of rose.

She was so beautiful in her discomfiture that

he was hard put to follow his sister and shut the door on her loveliness.

"What is it, Andy?" he asked, glancing back over his shoulder at the door.

Andromeda was wringing her hands together and studying him intently, and he soon focused his attention on her. "Whatever is wrong?" he asked, moving toward her.

"Nothing. Nothing is wrong. Miss Neville had some news to divulge this afternoon. Some important news."

She looked so worried that he immediately thought of the safety of all their friends. "Is her grandmother all right? Her mother? And Haven?"

"Yes, yes," she said, impatiently, flapping her bony hands around. "All are well. This was about herself. Colin, she has broken off her engagement to Lord Yarnell and he has eloped with another girl."

She spoke on, but Colin did not hear another word. He sat abruptly, lucky only that a chair was right there, since he did not plan it that way. She was not engaged anymore. Rachel was free. He took in a deep breath and let it out slowly, his head spinning.

"How did it happen?" He looked up at his sister and could tell he had interrupted her.

"I was just telling you. She told us that she found out he had a prior attachment, though there had been some split between him and the young lady, and so she broke off the engagement, freeing him to be with the one he loved. She told him to go to her!" She clasped her hands to her heart. "It is so romantic!"

"And is she all right?"

"She seems perfectly fine. In fact . . ." Andromeda paused and pursed her lips.

"What is it?"

"She seems . . . better. You know we have not been close these last several years. I have long thought her haughty and unpleasant. But I begin to think I have misjudged her."

Colin felt his breathing return to normal, and with it, skepticism returned. He had been blind to her faults for so long. He would not be oblivious again. "We shall see. It is perhaps just the shock of her broken engagement. And you must see that we are only hearing her side of the story. Inevitably it has been colored by her own perceptions. We will be guided by her behavior in the coming days."

"Well, I truly think she is different." Andromeda gave a sharp nod. "Better. Since her apology she has been steady in her amity, and that is new with Miss Neville. So, will you come to the ball tonight? Belinda is going to spend the evening up in the nursery entertaining the hostess's children, since their nursemaid is ill at the moment."

He thought about it and said, "I will come." It would give him a chance to observe this new Rachel. He did not want Andromeda hurt in any way, or publicly snubbed. He would see for himself this miraculous transformation.

They returned together to the parlor, and Rachel greeted the news with calm friendliness. "I am glad. I feel I have been remiss since you arrived. You will like the Lauriers. They are without pretension, truly lovely people."

Colin watched her for a few minutes as she returned to the pattern book with Belinda. She was edgy and nervous. When she stood to go, he followed her to the front hall.

"I will not pretend Andy did anything when we left the room but tell me of your new status, that you have released Lord Yarnell."

"And that he has eloped with Miss Danvers," Rachel said, with no rancor in her voice.

He put out one hand and touched her shoulder, but withdrew it after only the most fleeting of touches. "Are you all right? Was it truly your decision?" He gazed steadily into her eyes, trying to read her and failing, as usual. Her pale blue eyes were clear, though, so no night spent weeping, or the whites would be red and her eyes would be puffy.

"It was wholly my decision. Yarnell wished to go on with the marriage. He claimed Miss Danvers was not suitable, as she had her roots in trade."

"Stiff-rumped old parsnip! What changed his mind so suddenly?"

"I was not privy to the development, but I rather hope I did. I told him he would be a fool to turn his back on a love he so freely confessed and that he believed would last a lifetime."

He bit back his first impulse, which was to say that was strange advice, coming from a girl who had turned her back on love from him any number of times. He reminded himself that the love between Yarnell and Miss Danvers was mutual, while his had always been unrequited. And he had resolved that his was just habit, more out of routine than anything. And he would keep telling himself that until he could make his body and his heart believe it.

Rachel had turned away, and she said in a low

voice, "I may have need of all the friends I can find in the coming days. I shall be known as a jilt and as the girl who turned down a marquess, if people are even so kind as to leave it at that. I may be ridiculed, or even censured. I will most certainly be the object of gossip."

Perhaps this was why she was being so kind to them now, but if that was so, he could not find it in his heart to be angry. It touched him that she turned to them as to old friends. He placed his hand on her shoulder again, this time leaving it there and squeezing gently, and said, "You know you can count on us, Rachel."

She turned and her eyes were shining. "I know. That is my solace. I think I have learned what true friendship is, Colin. That lesson may be hammered home in the next days."

He longed to pull her close and knew in that moment that, far from being a chimera, his love for her was more real than ever, and perhaps insurmountable. Always he had been drawn to the vulnerable core he sensed under her sometimes brittle and haughty surface, and now, seeing her nervous and hearing her confession of reliance on them, he was more attracted than ever. But he would never be so foolish as to mistake her friendship for anything more, ever again. She would never be embarrassed by his unwanted attentions. He bid her good-bye as coolly as he was able, and she departed.

That night Colin escorted Andromeda and Belinda into the anteroom of the Lauriers' Chelsea residence and helped his sister off with her wrap.

A servant was dispatched to find out where Belinda was to go, but in the meantime the girl was peeking out from behind the curtained doorway at the ballroom. She was wholly engrossed.

Rachel joined them, pale and lovely in ice blue silk, a coronet of pearls in her dark hair. "I am so glad you have come," she said, her voice trembling as she reached out to Andromeda for a brief hug.

Colin, surprised by her friendly greeting of his sister, said, "Is everything as it should be, Rach . . . uh, Miss Neville?"

Blinking quickly, she said, "Oh, there have just been some rather unkind remarks already about Yarnell and Miss Danvers."

"You have done the right thing, and never forget it," Andromeda said, with her bracing tone. She had left behind her habitual headwear, a turban, and wore a simple headdress of pearls and feathers.

"Thank you," Rachel said with a watery smile. "Did you invite Sir Parnell, as you said you would?" she said, looking over at Colin.

"Sir Parnell?" Andromeda asked sharply. "Why would you invite Sir Parnell?"

Colin looked guilty. "Yes. He should be here any time. He doesn't have a very wide acquaintance in London, Andy, and I thought he might like to come and enjoy the party."

"And I did say gentlemen were in short supply," Rachel added. "Colin's note of inquiry about inviting Sir Parnell was quite welcome, and I know the Lauriers will be happy to see him. Many families are already starting to return to the country, you know, and good company is thinning out. The Season is almost over."

Lady Laurier entered and was introduced around. She was a pleasant, rotund woman just a few years older than Rachel. Belinda took to her motherly charm immediately, and bobbed off after her like a tiny skiff in a larger clipper's wake.

Colin offered his arms to both Rachel and Andromeda, and they entered the ballroom.

Rachel took a deep breath, relishing the comfort of Colin's strong arm clutching her close. It had been a difficult day. Her mother was not speaking to her, though there was every sign that she was somewhat relieved not to have to deal with Lady Yarnell again. Grand had come down ill and taken to her bed. That was completely unheard of, and Rachel found herself unexpectedly worried. It was lovely to have Colin to lean on and to have friends she knew she could depend upon to counter any nasty remarks that might come her way.

She introduced the Varenses to those of her friends she knew would not slight them. Sir Parnell Waterford arrived, exquisitely turned out for all that he was unfashionably brown, and he delighted all, charming several ladies completely with his tales of the exotic Caribbean. He then asked Andromeda for a dance. She had drawn herself up, and was about to say no, when Colin said yes for her and virtually pushed her into his arms. Rachel had watched with amusement, not sure whether Colin just wished them to be friends, or whether he was hoping for some other end. It was clear to her that Sir Parnell was fascinated by Andromeda, but men were ever dim on that subject, in her estimation, and she did not think Colin had any ulterior motive but a wish for his sister and friend to be on good terms.

She and Colin were standing together when an acquaintance of hers approached. As politeness demanded, even though this same girl had been one of the ones snickering about her broken engagement earlier, Rachel introduced Colin to her.

"Miss Edwina Staines-Frobisher, may I introduce to you Sir Colin Varens, an old neighbor and friend of mine."

Miss Staines-Frobisher demurely gave her hand and dropped a vague curtsy, then proceeded to flirt expertly, dropping her lashes whenever she looked directly at Colin and finding small opportunities to get close to him. Rachel watched in amazement, and when they were joined by two other young ladies who had not managed to find a beau who would commit his heart and earthly goods to them yet this late in the Season, she realized he was being viewed as fresh marriage material.

And when the feminine buzz around him was too overpowering and Rachel found she had been shouldered out of the way, Miss Connolly, a plain young woman with no airs or pretensions, sighed and gave up her place, joining Rachel to the side of the group.

"I suppose I may as well give up," she said. "He will never notice me with all of those girls around him."

"You want him to notice you?"

"I would like the opportunity!" she said, stoutly. "I must marry this year, for father says I shan't get a second London Season, no matter how shameful it is to have an unmarried daughter. We will go to Bath and I will be paraded in front of all the sick old men," she said, with a grimace. "Ugh! At least Sir Colin is young and . . ." She turned bright red, not being one who could blush gracefully. "Well, handsome."

"Colin, handsome?" Rachel blurted.

"Perhaps he is not a beau like Byron or Brummel, but he is . . ." She glanced around and whispered, "He is certainly well set-up, as my granny says!"

Rachel glanced over at the group of young ladies clustered around, Colin in the center, his broad shoulders and strong, homely face a masculine counterpoint to their feminine fragility. Even the stouter girls looked slender next to his muscular frame, and she realized that though he had used to be slender, he was considerably bulkier than he had been when younger.

It occurred to her in that moment that he could very well find a young lady to suit his fancy, for he had always been the kind who would be better and happier for a wife, she thought. For all that he was doing well in London, and fitting in better even at a ball than she would have believed possible, he was still most at home on a horse, riding his Yorkshire acreage.

Yes, Colin could find a wife, for there were certainly many ladies who seemed to find his unencumbered land and estate an attraction and, judging by Miss Connolly's words, who perhaps took a more personal interest in his strong young body and pleasant, courtly manner. As his friend, she should be happy for him that he was such a success. She certainly should be happy for him.

Thirteen

Andromeda Varens found herself on the dance floor and going through the steps of a familiar old country dance. Why the gentleman had asked her to dance was a mystery, and why Colin had pushed her into it another, but if it was to be so, she would utilize her time.

"Sir," she said, as they promenaded the floor after another couple in the intricate figures. "I wished to speak to you without my brother present, and it seems this may be my only opportunity."

"I am yours to command, Miss Varens," he said. He took her gloved hand in his and twirled her, turning them both perfectly, and they began their promenade in reverse direction.

"How do you happen to be so proficient at the dance, sir?" she asked, distracted by his elegant mastery. She had been afraid she would be out of practice and step on his toes, but it appeared that he was in easy control. "I thought you had been mired in the islands all these years."

His lean, dark face softened with a smile, the glint in his pale eyes humorous. "I like your choice of word, 'mired.' Do you not think English Society survives wherever there are English men and women?"

"Oh." She reflected on how little she knew about the islands. "Oh. I suppose I had not thought of it."

"No, you supposed me laboring in the fields with my workers, no doubt." He twirled her.

"You *are* very brown, sir," she said, breathlessly, gazing up at him.

"The Caribbean sun is relentless, scorching. It seeks you out, even with a hat on, even in the shade of a tree. Do you disapprove?"

She gazed up at his brown face, thinking his complexion was unfashionable, but at least he had done things in his life, worked and made something of himself. That was to be admired, in her estimation. "It is not to me to approve or disapprove your complexion, Sir Parnell," she said, sidestepping the issue. "And it is not what I wish to speak of."

"I follow your lead, ma'am."

He was holding her in the curve of his arm, and she lost what she was about to say in the novel sensation. The truth was, it had been many years since she had so much as danced with a gentleman . . . a *real* gentleman. Local assemblies in their Yorkshire village were more democratic than most, in the sense that all were welcome, from illustrious personages like Lord Haven and Sir Colin right down to the chandler and draper and any local farmer inclined to the lighthearted frivolity of dancing to a violin and piano. As much as she had heartily taken part in dancing with the people of her village, it was not quite the same as dancing with an eligible gentleman, perhaps because she knew that the draper and chandler were just looking for a jolly time, and their pleasure in the dance, as her own, must consist of how high they leapt or how speedy the steps.

Dancing with a gentleman was different, as she remembered from the last time she had waltzed with Lord Haven, their friend and neighbor. He was such a handsome man that her heart had beat faster, and her mind had imagined all kinds of fantastical conclusions to the dance, even down to a proposal on the dance floor.

But Haven had avoided her these many years, to her shame, because she had rather relentlessly pressured him to make her an offer. She had imagined herself in love with him because he was the man most suitable for her to wed in their limited social circle. For she had wanted to marry, to be mistress of her own house instead of keeping house for her brother, to have children—

"Miss Varens, the dance is ended."

Sir Parnell's gentle tone told her she had been woolgathering again, and she could feel the color rise above her modest neckline. "Ah. Yes."

"We have not yet had the conversation you wished to have. Would you walk with me on the terrace? We can talk more easily there than in the confines of a ballroom anyway."

She accepted his invitation and soon found herself enjoying the cooler breeze on the abbreviated terrace. Summer had blossomed with bountiful profusion, and the tiny terrace was crowded with potted plants and topiaries. Sir Parnell led her to a quiet corner between two topiary trees carved in an intricate spiral shape.

"Here . . . we can be private," he murmured.

A little too private, for her taste. With a muttered observation on the darkness, she moved them toward a beam of light from the window. He did not comment, merely moving as she did and staying close to her, close enough that she could still smell his spicy scent, something that made her think of the islands that were his home for so many years. 'Tall' and 'angular' had always been the phrases that were used by those trying to be kind in describing her, but Sir Parnell was even taller and more angular, standing a full head above her. He tucked her arm firmly under his and held it there as they stood on the stone parapet. Andromeda gazed at the moon, finding it hard to think of all the things she had wanted to upbraid him about.

"Miss Varens," he said, his voice hushed. "Do you know why I came back to England?"

"No." Her voice was unaccountably breathy.

"I missed this, this soft breeze, this view, civilization." He swept his free hand in an arc over the view of courtyards and walled gardens lit with a hundred fairy lights. "This city. I have always loved London, for all of its quirks and follies."

"Like dying climbing boys and foul air and poverty and gin-soaked mothers and . . ."

"Do you think colonial society did not have its fair share of pain and sorrow? The islands attract a poor class of Englishman, I am afraid. The dissolute, the weak, gamblers, thieves, wastrels, all think the islands will conceal their abundant folly. But weakness is weakness, and the islands have no magic cure."

"Did *you* go there to escape your own weaknesses?"

He chuckled. "A worthy question, I suppose. No, I went to escape poverty and make my fortune."

"So why did you come back?"

He sighed. "I found it impossible to stay after a time. I made my fortune, and then could no longer wink at the terrible consequences of colonialism. Slavery continues to be a blight on our civilization. We benefit from it, even if we pretend we disapprove." He looked off still over the gardens below, squinting a little, the wrinkles at the corners of his eyes crinkling. "We have abolished the sale of men and women into slavery, but every day children are born into that state. I . . . owned slaves myself, but I found that it was corroding my soul."

Andromeda could not breathe. She moved away from him. "You owned slaves?" She knew her voice betrayed her disgust.

"I am not proud of that fact, but as a youth I thought only of making my mark in the world. The colonies are the surest place for a young man of little wealth but much ambition to find his fortune."

"And now you have the luxury of conscience?" she said, acidly.

"If you wish to characterize it thus, yes. Maybe that is so. I did not even think about it at first, owning slaves. It was what everyone did." His expression in the dimness of the moonlit terrace hardened, and his stare was challenging. "But remember this when you put sugar in your tea and clothe yourself in cotton muslin: just because there are no slaves in London parlors, do not think we can look down our noses and say we are superior. If . . . or, rather *when* all slavery is abolished, as I hope it soon will be, we—English society—will be in an uproar, for our cotton and sugar and rum will become prohibitively expensive. That will be the test of our morals."

Andromeda frowned. There was too much to think of in his words, too many moral judgments to make, and far too much reason to believe them all culpable, not just those who owned slaves. She remained silent.

His expression softened, and so did his voice. "But all of life everywhere has such things to be ashamed of as humans who share this world. The slaves are slaves because their brethren on the African continent sold them to the slavers. They own slaves themselves, you know, the Africans. That does not pardon our shame, though. Someday I will tell you the story of the day I changed from a believer in the institution of slavery to one who abhors the practice. It is not a pretty story, but you are an intelligent woman, not one of these silly little butterflies afraid of the truth. I will just say that one chooses carefully what battles one has the energy and wherewithal to fight, and then one engages the enemy, if that is what one wishes to do. But one man—or woman—cannot fight them all. I have come back to England to do what I can about the plight of the slaves and their children. That is my battle, and I have chosen carefully and thought long on the subject."

She thought about what he said and nodded. "You are right. In my limited sphere as a woman, and an unmarried one at that, I have chosen education for the children of Lesleydale as what I can effect a transformation on." She shivered and rubbed her arms. "There is change in the air, and the cottagers cannot depend on their looms anymore, nor is one man's farm enough to feed his family. They must learn and grow. Education is the cure to so many ills."

"And you care? You care about the poor children?"

There was an odd tone in his voice, and she felt if she knew him better, she would understand the meaning behind it. She met his gaze steadily in the dim light cast from the ballroom window. "If you do not care about something, you are dead inside. I have no husband, nor do I have children. I must care about something." She had never spoken so to anyone, and could not understand what had possessed her to speak so bluntly to a stranger.

"You are young yet." His tone was gentle, and he reached out one hand to caress her neck. "You will wed and have children, I am sure of it."

She looked up at his dark face in the moonlight. With him, for some reason, honesty came easily to her lips. He did not need to know the humiliations she had suffered, nor the disappointments when she had thought herself close to finding a mate, but he would know her resolve in that direction. "I have made peace with the notion that I will never marry now. I will care for my brother's house, and when he marries, retire to a cottage in the village. I struggled against it for so long, but now I know it will be all right. Life will go on. And I am not so young, Sir Parnell. Thirty-one is not young."

"Nor is forty-three, but the path of our life is not cut until we walk it. I may yet find a lady . . ."

He had faltered and she gazed up at him, wondering what was wrong. He was staring at her with an odd expression in his pale eyes, and she thought that perhaps he did not believe his own words. She ached for him, and for the loneliness in his voice.

But enough. She had come out here to speak of Colin, and instead had ended up talking of everything but. She straightened her spine and lifted her chin.

"I wish to speak with you about Colin, Sir Parnell." If honestly indeed came so easily with the gentleman, then she would speak what was on her mind. "I would have you stop this boxing idiocy and tell Colin to quit now, before he gets hurt."

He sighed. "I can't do that, Miss Varens."

"Not *can't.* Won't. You *won't* do anything. Please be honest with me, at least."

"All right, I will." He leaned back against the terrace wall and crossed his arms across his chest. "Whether I train him or not, your brother will box. He did it before I took him on and will continue even if I tell him I will no longer train him. With my guidance, he may fight safely and only engage with other trained boxers willing to fight by Broughton's Rules of Conduct."

"Rules? In a fight?" Andromeda felt anger well up at his obstinacy.

"Yes, rules. Do you know, in fights in which no rules are held to be necessary, men have had eyes gouged out and . . ." He paused and stared at her, aghast, reaching out to steady her with one brown hand. "Miss Varens, you have gone white! I am so sorry for saying such a thing. I just wish . . . if you could but once see us practice . . ."

"I do not need to see brutality to know what is

brutal." Andromeda pulled away. "I wish to return to my brother, sir."

"Of course. Immediately."

The knight's words had vividly depicted one of her worst fears, and Andromeda could not listen to more. They entered and crossed the ballroom floor, weaving between dancers and circumventing a line of watchers. But as they approached the crowd of young ladies, in the center of which Colin, smiling and chatting, stood, she turned and gazed up at her companion. "If you have any conscience, you will turn Colin away. Stop him from taking part in this foolhardiness. He is precious to me, and I do not wish to see him hurt."

"For your sake, Miss Varens, if I thought it would stop him, I would turn him away. How could I resist the plea of a sister who so clearly loves her brother? But I fear that if I turn Sir Colin away, he will only seek out those of the stamp who beat him so badly when he tried to find a match on his own. I can train him properly and find for him fitting combatants. It will serve your needs better if I go on with the training. I pledge to you that I will do all in my power to see to his safety, and I believe I will accomplish that by making him the best pugilist he can be."

Andromeda primmed her lips into a tight line. Perhaps he was right that she should see Colin box. Knowing the enemy was the first step in any battle, and she knew little or nothing about pugilism, by choice. But watching Colin train was not going to tell her anything. She needed to see the real thing, a true match. She nodded. Yes, she very much feared she would need to find an ally in her desperate battle to save Colin from himself.

Colin felt as if his smile was so tight, it was like the grimace of a death mask. He could make no sense of what any lady said anymore, for they all spoke at once, chattering like magpies. Rachel had disappeared, and he saw no polite way to disperse the crowd of young ladies. What to do?

He saw Andromeda and Sir Parnell approach and reached out to them as though they were a lifeline and he a drowning man.

"My sister, ladies, and Sir Parnell Waterford. Sir Parnell, I believe you have many exciting tales to tell of your successful venture as a planter in the islands of the Caribbean!"

It sounded so patently forced that for a moment he thought no one would take the bait, but these were young ladies who had yet to make a conquest, and so Sir Parnell was fallen upon like fresh strawberries at a picnic. They crowded around him.

Colin took his sister's arm, and with a babbled request to be excused while he discussed something with his sister, he led her away.

"Do not look back," he said, pulling her along with him until they reached the edge of the ballroom floor. When they had put enough distance between them and those left behind, he allowed their pace to slow and passed one hand over his eyes. "What has come over the so called fair sex? I have never seen so many fluttering eyelashes and heaving . . . yes, well . . ." He glanced at his sister. "I shall just say it is highly uncomfortable to be the center of so much concentrated flirtation. What has happened? Have I suddenly become a beau that I am treated to so much female attention?"

Andromeda chuckled. "No, you will never be a beau. But it is the end of the Season, and you are an unclaimed bachelor of a good age and with an unencumbered estate and only one female relative. You are a prize, of sorts, to those who have not managed to find a husband and are becoming, for want of a better word, desperate."

Colin let out a shout of laughter. "And I thought I had suddenly become handsome and witty. No one like one's sister for letting one down easily." He gave her a sly look. "Now I know how Haven felt all those years when you were trying so desperately to entrap him."

She pinched his arm hard and steered him toward their hostess. He yelped, but kept grinning. When they reached Lady Laurier, Andromeda said, "My lady, we have become separated from Miss Neville. Have you seen her?"

"Oh, yes," Lady Laurier said, with an ingenuous smile on her pretty face. "Miss Neville is quite the belle of the ball! She is an enormous success with the young gentlemen. Would you like me to guide you to her?"

Colin was flushed a deep red and said, stiffly, "Yes, we would be obliged."

Andromeda glanced sideways at him. She thought he had found equanimity where Rachel Neville was concerned. The lady had rejected him often enough, certainly, and he seemed to have finally realized there would never be anything between them. But he looked stricken at the idea of her at the center of a group of gentlemen. "Is this wise?" she murmured, but he did not appear to hear.

Their hostess led them along a passageway and up some back stairs. Where could they possibly be going? Another set of stairs, and Andromeda began to wonder how Miss Neville, the most correct of young ladies, could have allowed herself to be so separated from the safety of the gathering.

Pressing one gloved finger to her lips, Lady Laurier led them down another passage. She opened a doorway and beckoned to them to look inside. Colin's face was grim, and Andromeda approached with trepidation. She peeked inside with her brother.

Seated in a comfortable chair, Rachel Neville, her gloves stripped off and discarded, sat in a comfortable chair with a baby cradled in her lap and a little boy sleeping next to her, his thumb stuck firmly in his mouth. Belinda was sitting in another chair with a little girl of about five years curled up next to her, and she was reading aloud while Rachel, her eyes closed, stroked the little boy's golden curls. It was a scene of domestic bliss that Andromeda would never have expected from Miss Rachel Neville. When she turned to say as much to Colin, she was struck by his expression.

His homely face had softened, and there was such tenderness there that her heart ached. For she knew it had nothing to do with the beautiful Laurier children and everything to do with the much more beautiful Rachel Neville. Her poor brother was just as besotted as he always had been, no matter what he might say or think.

Miss Neville opened her eyes just then, and

they gleamed softly with yearning. "Oh, Colin, Andromeda, is this not the most beautiful sight in the world?"

"Yes, it is," Colin said. He dragged in a deep breath. "I have never seen anything more enchanting in my whole life."

Fourteen

"Mother, you cannot keep ignoring me. It will do no good." Rachel watched her mother for a moment, but the woman was deliberately not meeting her eyes.

"I do not speak to ungrateful children, and you are ungrateful." Lady Haven was seated at the dining room table looking over a letter.

Rachel knew what it was. Lady Haven had reached some peace concerning Rachel's jilting of Lord Yarnell and his subsequent elopement. It helped immeasurably that she despised Lady Yarnell so thoroughly. But that was not to say it still did not sting that she had had a daughter on the verge of wedding a marquess in a highly public, completely suitable ceremony in London.

And every once in a while something would remind her of all that they had lost with Yarnell's rejection. Rachel knew what it was that had triggered this bout of anguish. She had heard at length about the letter her mother had received the day before from Haven, her only son, *another* ungrateful child, as their mother styled them. He had eloped just a month or so before rather than enjoy the glorious London wedding she was planning for him and his fiancée. The eager couple had eloped to Yorkshire and were living on the Haven estate, but not at magnificent, ancient Haven Court. Instead, at the new Lady Jane Haven's request, they were cozily occupying a cottage on the grounds. His letter spoke no apology, though, for their rash behavior in forgoing the grandeur of a London wedding. Instead he gushed immodestly of how happy he was, how perfect his life, and how wonderful his wife.

Lady Lydia Haven could not even think about the missed opportunity to celebrate the ancient and noble title of Lord Haven in a suitable wedding, displaying to the *ton* the grandeur of their splendid line, without becoming choleric. She was livid with fury over her son's ingratitude to his mother for all of her labor to create the perfect wedding for the Haven name. But in the end, after much debate on both sides, he had chosen to honor his wife-to-be's wishes over those of his mother, and had carried Jane north to marry hastily and enjoy the fruits of his marriage in bucolic peace. Society was snickering, Lady Lydia felt sure, behind their fans and gloved hands.

And now Rachel had rejected a suitor she had chosen herself, with no prompting from her mother, and all for some unfathomable scruples about the gentleman's past love life. Incomprehensible. Her children were most certainly a flock of mockingbirds in the familial nest, for they surely were not her own offspring, to be so cavalier about the important things in life: status, wealth, a good settlement, and the proper and elaborate display of all of the aforementioned. That Pamela's wedding had been celebrated in London was not even to be mentioned, for it was a hasty thing, accomplished within two weeks of the proposal instead of two months.

Rachel knew the labyrinthine pathways of her mother's resentment because before she had stopped speaking to her daughter, the area had been well canvassed. She let the subject drop. Just a month or so before, she would have agreed wholeheartedly with her mother and could not begin to explain the strange changes that were taking place in her heart. "I am going to sit with Grandmother for a while, and then I have promised Miss Varens and Belinda that I will accompany them to a poetry reading."

Lady Haven snorted, but it was followed by a quick frown. "Your grandmother . . . ask her if she needs anything. I will see that Cook makes her a beef broth for her luncheon, if she will just try to take some of it."

Rachel, rising from the table, paused and sat back down, watching her mother's lined face. "You aren't worried about her, are you?"

"She's over eighty," Lady Haven said with apparent asperity, staring down at the letter—her ungrateful son's missive—and folding one corner of it over and over. "She's outlived her usefulness. Time and past that she should go to her reward."

"Mother," Rachel said, sharply. "Just admit you are worried about Grandmother. Why can you not do that?"

The woman shrugged, then her shoulders dropped, and she slumped. "I have known her for almost thirty-four years. I cannot imagine what will happen when she . . . when she goes."

"I know. She is so strong." Rachel was silent for a moment, wondering how to ask what she wanted to know. "But . . . pardon me, Mother. You two always seemed to dislike each other so. And you bicker constantly. Will you not at least enjoy some peace once she is gone?"

"I suppose." She tossed the letter aside and clasped her hands together, staring at them, her lips working as if she were fighting some strong emotion. "But I would rather not have that peace yet." She swallowed hard and cleared her throat. Her gaze became unfocused, as though she were looking back on some past scene. "I will never forget when . . . when I was very ill and lost a child. I was devastated. I pray you never suffer that torment, Rachel. She was a rock—not like your father, who just closed himself off and would not speak to me. He never could bear illness, coward that he was."

Lady Haven had always spoken disparagingly of her husband, and Rachel resisted the urge to lash out. Her father had been dear to Rachel, and yet she must live with her mother the way she was, not how she would wish she was. It was a hard-learned lesson.

"She gave me the strength to go on," Lady Haven said, squeezing her eyes shut. "She knew just what to say, as she had been through it herself more than once. I have been thinking of that a lot these last few days. I have been thinking of all those times I had forgotten, when she was there when no one else was."

Rachel had no answer and did not think one was required. She left her mother alone, head bowed, at the table and went to her grandmother's room with a renewed sense that life was a mystery. Her mother had always been a closed book to her, distant, difficult, abrasive. But the fear on her face as she acknowledged that losing her mother-in-law would be a sad day made Rachel realize that no person or emotional attachment could be categorized or easily explained. She would never be able to express it, she knew, but she felt a tenderness toward her mother, seeing a vulnerable side to a hard and difficult woman.

The dowager was pale and her breathing was shallow, though she was sleeping deeply. Rachel told the maid who was sitting with the woman to go and have her breakfast—or, rather, luncheon, more likely.

Rachel sat down in the bedside chair and covered her grandmother's hand on the coverlet with one of her own, examining the contrast between the knobby white blue-veined hand and her own smooth and young one. "I will miss you, too, when you do decide to go. But I don't believe you *will* go this time. I still need you, Grand, and so does Mother." She squeezed the hand that lay so still and closed her eyes, saying a little prayer.

Silence fell in the dim room. It was the only bedroom on the ground level of the ugly Haven town house, and so the sounds of the house could be heard beyond the door, the bustling of servants, a knock at the front door, voices. But in the dowager's room it was muffled.

"What should I be doing with my life now, Grandmother?" Her voice echoed strangely. "You told me to just enjoy my time, but I don't think I know how. I am so accustomed to having a purpose to form my days. Shall I become a spinster like Andromeda? I don't think so, since I do not believe I have even her inner resources. I shall dwindle into a pettish, unhappy old woman." She sighed, and then frowned at the self-pity she heard in her own voice. "How idiotic! I will do no such thing, and I know you will be there so I do not."

A tap at the door, and Andromeda Varens slipped in quietly.

"How is your grandmother?" she said, approaching the bed.

"Sleeping."

"Best thing for her. I brought a jar of calf's foot jelly; good for what ails her. So nutritious, and yet palatable even for an invalid. Lady Haven said she would make sure she had some at luncheon."

Rachel heard tension in the woman's voice and thought perhaps something was wrong, but she would wait until they were away from her grandmother's bedside. "That is very kind of you."

Andromeda looked the woman over with an expert eye. "Hmm, I think she will recover from this," she said.

"Do you think so?" Rachel asked. "How do you know?"

"Her breathing. I have attended many bedsides of those who are passing on, and have noted a similarity of wind; impossible to explain, really."

Rachel examined the older woman curiously as she bent over the sleeping dowager, listening and watching, her sharp, dark eyes knowledgeably sliding over the invalid. As a child, she had been grateful for Andromeda Varens's care, especially during that two-month period when Pamela was sick and Rachel was banished to Corleigh, the Varens's estate.

So how had she gone from that state of respect and affection to the almost enmity that had existed between them these last years? She knew she had changed when her father died. It had felt like going into a long, dark tunnel, and when she came out the other end she was not the same person. She felt frozen and distant from life, separated even from those she loved. And yet she had no one to talk to about it, no one to tell how she missed her father, and how lonely she felt.

It was an awful time at Haven Court. Her grandmother had just lost her only child, and her mother had lost her husband. They were wholly consumed with arrangements and services and finances. Visitors streamed to the estate, and there were letters of sympathy to answer. Her brother was adjusting to the importance and duties of his new title. Pamela was so very young, just a child who didn't wholly understand. Rachel had felt alone in her overwhelming grief for the one family member who had adored her above everyone else.

Perhaps if she had turned to Andromeda, things would have been different. Instead she withdrew from everyone. Then a few years later Colin had begun to court her. Flattered at first, and willing to practice her flirting on him, she had not turned him away resolutely. Seeing it fresh from Andromeda's view, she must have seemed like a jade to lead him to think there was a possibility that she would marry him, only to finally say no when he offered, and then to repeatedly and with increasing sharpness turn him away. A sister's partiality would find no reason for her rejection of him.

Andromeda finally took a seat, sighing. "Yes, I really do think your grandmother will come out of this. I fear she will be weak for a long time, though. The best thing for her would be fresh air, but there is precious little to be had in London, I am afraid."

"Should we take her back to Yorkshire immediately?"

"She won't be ready to make such an arduous journey for some time, I think. At least a month or so."

"Oh. Where is Belinda?"

"With Lady Haven."

Rachel's eyes widened, but Andromeda, seeing that, said, "I warned Belinda that your mother can be . . . difficult, and told her to be on her best behavior."

"Even that will not help, not in her present mood. I am afraid my broken engagement following upon my brother's elopement has affected her in an adverse manner."

"It seems to me—pardon, Miss Neville, for my bluntness—that your mother can be just as difficult in a fine mood as she can be in a troublesome one."

They both saw the dowager's lips curve up in a smile. Rachel wondered if she was awake and listening, or if it was just a random occurrence indicating that she was dreaming.

Andromeda merely smiled and turned back to Rachel. "Before we go this afternoon to the poetry reading, I wished to speak to you alone, Miss Neville—Rachel—about a matter of some importance to me."

"Speak on . . . uh, Andromeda," Rachel said, trying to not sound awkward. They had been on first name terms many years before, but had gotten out of the habit. Surely now, as adults and neighbors, and now as friends, they should be able to return to that friendly footing.

Andromeda shifted uneasily on her chair. She fiddled with her gown and folded the material between her gloved fingers. "You know how concerned I am about Colin's new pastime, boxing. Sir Parnell has been training him, and now they have scheduled a match. Try as I might, I can persuade neither of them to stop this foolishness and find some safer way to spend their days."

Rachel shrugged. "Men will be men. If they want to spend their time battering each other senseless, what are women to do?"

"If it were anyone else but my brother, I would concur. Men are unfathomable a great deal of the time; the things they think are important, the joy they take in senseless activities! However, I fear for Colin's safety, and cannot hold my tongue in this instance." She took a deep breath and met Rachel's gaze. "You are perhaps too young to remember, or your mother kept the information from you, but several years ago a fellow died boxing in Lesleydale."

"Died?"

"Yes. From what I heard, he seemed to be just fine after a fight in which he took several blows to the head, but then later he began to complain of a headache, and then he fell down in a fit and passed away."

Shocked, Rachel remained silent, watching Andromeda's gloved hands twisting around and around each other.

Finally, Andromeda spoke again, urgently, leaning forward, her words tumbling over each other like fretful acrobats. "I cannot just sit idly by while my brother pursues a course that I feel will end in disaster."

"But what can you do?" Rachel asked, feeling helpless. "He is a man, and will do what he wants."

"I don't know. But I do know that the first rule of engagement is that one must study the enemy, learn all one can about that which one must combat." She seemed unaware of the irony inherent in her combative words.

"And what does that mean in this instance?"

"It means I must ask a favor. I feel that even though there have been . . . incidences between Colin and yourself, that you do care for him as a friend. Am I right about that?"

Rachel felt the flush rise in her cheeks. Andromeda's eyes were shrewd. Many people did not see beyond her romanticism and her resolute chase after Lord Haven for so many years and thought she was just an eccentric spinster. But when she was passionate about a subject, she was fiercely committed. It would be a mistake to underestimate her intelligence.

"Of course you are right. Colin and I have cried friends now that he has gotten over his ridiculous infatuation." It was said stiffly, and Rachel hoped Andromeda did not take offense.

"Then help me stop this. Help me find out the truth about these boxing matches," Andromeda urged. "Sir Parnell has Colin in a match two nights from tonight, his first. Let's see for ourselves what brutality men inflict on one another."

"You mean . . ."

"I mean we should dress as gentlemen and see the match."

Fifteen

The club dedicated to the promotion of pugilistic arts—an adjunct of the Apollonian Club and jokingly referred to as the Olympian—was a nondescript house on a nondescript street in the heart of a decent neighborhood. Nothing distinguished it from the other houses on the block, except for the carriages arriving and dispersing gentlemen only. Inside it was much the same. The front rooms were dedicated to normal club business: smoking, drinking, and gambling. Only once one got past these rooms did one became aware of a difference.

Three rooms had been thrown together to create a large open area, with chandeliers giving considerable light. A ring was chalked on a low stage in the center of the room, and men were crowded around, money changing hands, muttered discussions taking place, and ribald jokes passing from one to another. On evenings with a fight scheduled, rather than the impromptu bouts that often took place, the doors were open to anyone who wished to attend and gamble.

Tonight's match had not caused much talk until it was known that Sir Parnell Waterford had trained and was backing the untried fighter. He was boxing against the current favorite, Sussex Sam, a young fellow who had once been a footman, and who stood a strapping six feet tall, a veritable giant among the general populace of men.

Men whispered back and forth. Who was this young fellow Sir Parnell was backing? The knight had a reputation for taking on no one who did not show great natural potential. So should the odds be better for the fellow, rumored to be a baronet, though no one was quite sure? Surely Sam would trounce him. But p'raps a few pounds on the other fellow, just to cut their losses in case Cutthroat Colin turned out to be a good 'un.

Three young gentlemen, one clearly some years older than the other two, sidled into the room and strolled arm in arm, nonchalantly sizing up the crowd. One murmured to the other, and they made sure to keep the youngest, a mere cub, close at hand in the densely smoky den.

The ring was set, the square in the middle chalked for the combatants to step up to, and the crowd took on an air of hushed expectancy, last minute wagers fiercely whispered. The bout was to start any minute.

Rachel, dressed in an ill-fitting suit of clothes, felt sure that at any moment someone would denounce her for the fraud she was and they would be rudely manhandled . . . or worse! What had she been thinking to let Andromeda talk her into such a monumentally idiotic undertaking? And what was the woman doing bringing Belinda?

"I feel sure we should not have brought Belinda," she whispered to her taller companion, who looked like a very proper—if a little too smooth skinned—gentleman.

"She swore she would not stay at home while we were out having larks," Andromeda muttered, leaning down to speak to Rachel. "I reasoned that better she should be here under our guardianship than sneaking in alone. She is quite capable of it, you know."

Remembering shocking stories of Belinda's past escapades in the year since her parents' tragic death in a carriage accident, Rachel had to agree that, given the situation, Andromeda had judged best.

Given the situation. Given that two adult ladies of good breeding were dressed in gentlemen's togs and attending a boxing match.

Ridiculous. The situation was ridiculous and *they* were in imminent danger of becoming ridiculous by their actions.

It had sounded well enough in theory. Andromeda had been persuasive, and Rachel was willing to be persuaded. Her little sister, Pamela, had always been the one to have larks; well, now Rachel would have stories to tell her now-married younger sister about her own adventures.

But Andromeda had been serious about her quest to learn all she could about boxing so she could dissuade or otherwise stop Colin from participating in boxing matches. When questioned closely, the woman did not really have a plan in mind, but just to observe and learn. Rachel could not imagine what they would learn that would give Andromeda the ammunition to convince Colin to abandon something he so clearly enjoyed, but now that they were there, she decided she might as well do what they had come for.

Belinda was bright eyed and enjoying the experience. She tugged on Rachel's sleeve after a moment, and whispered something that Rachel could not hear for the din. She leaned closer to the girl, and Belinda repeated her words.

"Over there . . . there is Miss Pamela's friend Dexter!"

"Oh, wonderful," Rachel groaned. "Someone who knows us! As if it is not bad enough that we need conceal ourselves in this hideous fashion! How do men wear these things?" Breeches chafed on the tender skin between the thighs, she found, when one was not accustomed to them. Or perhaps it was just that these fit ill, binding in all the wrong places and loose where they should not be. It made her pink to even think of her unmentionable limbs, but the constant chafing would let her think of little else. And the tight binding across her chest left her breathless.

This was going to be a disaster. She felt it in her bones.

But Andromeda, her dark eyes sparkling with an odd excitement given that she was there to condemn and disapprove, was oblivious. A man stepped into the ring and announced the fight between Sussex Sam and Cutthroat Colin was about to begin.

Cutthroat Colin? Rachel would have giggled if such a feminine sound would not give her away.

And then a giant stepped up, and she had no more urge to giggle. At least he seemed a giant to Rachel. He was a big man, six feet at least, and bulky. His shoulders were broad and his forearms the size of hams. This was Colin's opponent? Sam's 'second,' a squat older man, chattered at him and the giant listened intently, nodding. His eyes swept the crowd and for one instant rested on Rachel. She shrank back, sure this was the moment that she would be denounced, but the man merely gazed at her for a moment and then let his gaze travel over the rest of the throng.

Then Sir Parnell stepped into the ring, followed by Colin. Shorter than his opponent by at least four inches, Colin at least matched him in breadth, for although he was slim at the waist, he sharply broadened at the shoulders. Rachel could not take her eyes from her old friend. It was as though she had been wearing blinkers for all these years, and now they were off. The admiration of the girls at the ball two evenings before had started the work, she supposed, and this finished it, seeing the deadly seriousness on his homely, lantern-jawed face, his dark eyes staring out from pale skin sheened already with sweat.

This was not the mild, almost meek suitor who for years had agreed with every silly phrase she uttered and who proposed every spring and autumn, as regular as the vernal and autumnal equinoxes. This was a dark-eyed stranger, a man not to be dallied with. The slow steady thud of her heart quickened.

Sir Parnell helped him off with his shirt and Rachel felt an odd gurgle in the pit of her stomach, spellbound by the first sight of a shirtless Colin, sinewy, corded muscles standing out like taut ropes under his skin. Even his stomach was muscled with sleek bulges, and an arrow of dark

hair narrowed and disappeared in the tight waist-
band of breeches that clung to his sturdy limbs. An
odd buzzing in her ears drowned out the sound
around her. Andromeda grasped her arm and
hauled her closer through the tight gathering of
men, and Rachel stumbled along behind her companion, her breath coming in strange little gasps.

She had thought they were to wear 'mufflers,'
a kind of glove that protected the hands from
abuse and the face and body from bare-knuckled
hits. Awakened from her stupor by Andromeda's
rough treatment, she whispered as much to Andromeda, who shrugged.

"That is what I was told they did, but perhaps
that is just for practice. I did not think to ask if
they also wore them in the actual bout." Her
voice was tight with anxiety.

Tension in the room was building. The buzzing
of voices intensified, and more money exchanged
hands now that both combatants had been seen.

Belinda, oblivious to her companions' distress,
was hopping up and down, trying to see the ring,
which was chalked off on a stage raised only a
foot or two off the floor. A gentleman in front of
them said, "Hey, young lad, want to see better?
Take the spot in front of me."

Before Rachel could protest, the girl had done
it. She was still in view, though, so Andromeda
shrugged and whispered that she supposed it
would be all right.

A fellow dressed in a snuff-stained jacket in an
improbable shade of green stepped up and
waved his arms around. The crowd fell silent. He
announced the bout, and said that everyone
must stop crowding the stage and step off imme-

diately, as the bout was to begin without further delay. He ordered Sir Parnell and the fellow with Sussex Sam off the stage, too.

The fight began with a shouted order from the announcer.

Rachel could see Colin only from about the waist up, as the men in front of her were taller than she. It was infuriating, she found, because all she could see were the jabs and upper movements, when she felt drawn to see the entire fight.

Blood pounded in her ears, and the huzzahs and cheering of the crowd of men for their favorite—most appeared to have money on Sam—were deafening. Rachel pushed through the crowd and found a spot near the stage by Belinda.

Colin, deadly intent, was holding his own quite well against the bigger man since he was faster, his feints and parries much like his expertise with a sword, which was no mean accomplishment. He landed a blow, and his opponent roared with pain, his lip curling in a snarl like a cornered beast. Rachel was petrified. She clutched Belinda to her side, and felt the girl shiver too. Or was that herself?

Sussex Sam landed a telling blow on Colin's chin, and he staggered, reeling backward. Rachel gasped, but Colin surged forward again, sending his fist into the other man's taut stomach muscles. It must have been a hard blow, for the man doubled over. Colin delivered another, but his opponent was not done yet. Perhaps he had underestimated the newcomer to the ring, for a look of more concentrated fury hardened his ugly, scarred face, and he redoubled his efforts to beat Colin.

Rachel could see Sir Parnell at the other side of the ring, his dark face intent, flinching with every blow landed on his pupil. He shouted commands, telling Colin to tuck, to feint, to parry, to jab. As blow after blow landed, sweat began to splatter the crowd and a fleck of blood appeared at the corner of Sussex Sam's cut mouth.

A pause was called. Sir Parnell and Sam's squat second leaped into the ring with cloths and water. They wiped down their fighters and talked to them. Colin listened and glanced at the other man, then listened again and nodded.

Rachel's heartbeat was just returning to normal as she tried to conceal her and Belinda's presence by turning their backs to the ring and hunching over, but the pause was over in a second, it seemed, and the bout started again. She turned, unable to keep her gaze from the fight, and watched.

Colin, unbelievably, appeared to be winning. He was relentless; no blow fazed him. She found herself cheering, and clamped her mouth shut, knowing her feminine voice would give her away even among men who were staring only at the fighters. She pressed a fist to her mouth to keep herself silent, but unable to restrain her exuberance and stop from jumping up and down, clutching Belinda.

But then he took a blow to the head and staggered sideways, caught off balance. He steadied himself, but another blow followed.

Rachel screamed, and in that one second, as Colin's head whipped around and his gaze found her in the crowd, Sam took advantage of his opponent's wandering attention and hit him so hard strings of spittle and blood flew out and hit the spectators. Colin reeled and fell to his knees, and then backward.

Colin! He was hurt!

Sam stepped back and waited for the arbitrator to jump into the ring, but he was not as quick as Rachel. Ducking under the loose rope that delineated the edge of the ring, feeling her hat fly off but not caring, Rachel scrambled across the sweat-slicked surface of the ring floor and bent over Colin, shrieking his name as she saw blood stream from his mouth. "Colin," she sobbed, her tears falling onto his cheeks. His eyes fluttered open, and their gazes met for one brief moment as the crowd yelled and pounded on the stage.

She was about to pull him to her, but felt herself abruptly hauled to her feet and shoved out of the ring. Unceremoniously, she was grasped under her arms and dragged out of the room. Her immediate reaction was to kick and scream, but as though at a distance she heard Andromeda say, "Rachel, shut up! It is Sir Parnell who has you. We must get out of here. You have given us away!"

The next few moments were a blur, but soon she was sitting in a carriage with Andromeda and Belinda on their way back to the Strongwycke London house where the Varenses and Belinda were staying. Her man's jacket was in disarray, her carefully tied mathematical loose, and her hair tumbled out of its tight coiffure, which had been hidden under a curl-brimmed beaver.

She was a mess.

And she didn't care.

"Colin . . . how is he?" She sat up straight.

"Wasn't that a bully fight?" Belinda said, eagerly sitting on the edge of the carriage seat.

Andromeda, seated across from them, shook her head with a mournful expression on her handsome face. "You would think at my age I would know better. I should have done this alone."

"I am sorry for spoiling your adventure, Andromeda," Rachel said, "but . . ."

"Don't be ridiculous. I am not angry at you," she replied, her tone rueful, "but at myself. What I was thinking to take a beautiful young lady and a girl child, when I could clearly see that neither of you were the faintest bit convincing, whereas I, unfortunately, can very easily pass as a gentleman."

"But we would have gotten away with it if Rachel hadn't shrieked and leaped on Sir Colin!" Belinda was giggling, and sat back against the squabs roaring with laughter, holding her stomach. "That was so funny! The rope knocked your hat off, Miss Neville, and your hair came loose and streamed down your back and . . ."

Andromeda put up one ungloved hand and said, "Belinda, you needn't repeat the whole . . ."

"No, let her," Rachel said, wearily. "I remember nothing from the time I leaped into the ring, except poor Colin's battered face, and that was my own fault! He heard me cry out, looked over at me, and that brute sunk his fist into his chin. It was horrible."

Andromeda was watching her, curiosity lighting up her dark eyes. "So that is what made him lose his concentration. I wondered. I thought he might win before that."

"So did I," Rachel answered, and set about tidying herself.

Thinking back over the evening, from the moment Colin first stepped into the ring and stripped off his shirt, Rachel thought it was as if some strange spirit had taken her over. She had felt hot and cold in turn, and her stomach had never ceased an unladylike rumbling, just as her whole body shivered. It had been as if she was possessed, her physical reactions were so unexpected.

What was wrong with her? Why had she reacted as she did? The fight, with Colin performing so magnificently, his muscular frame taut with brute force and his fists flailing, had excited her in some odd way that she was not particularly keen to explore. She feared it reflected poorly on her ladylike demeanor.

But when she had seen Colin go down, toppling like a stone, it had felt like a piece of her was being torn into shreds. The only explanation she could come up with was that all of the anticipation had made her the shivering muddle she had been, and that seeing her friend hurt had been all she could take, making her break out in her emotional outburst.

That had to be the explanation.

She said that to Andromeda, and the other woman nodded. "That must be it," she said, smiling. "Yes, indeed, you have most certainly offered a logical explanation for your behavior." There was an inscrutable expression on her lean face, though, as if she had a secret.

"I hope Colin is all right," Rachel said, trying to ignore Andromeda's odd behavior. "Please tell him to come see me tomorrow. I need to know that he has suffered no ill effects from my poorly timed outburst."

"I will most certainly tell him to come and see you tomorrow," Andromeda said, again with that odd smile.

"Good." She frowned at the other woman's intent gaze, and then looked away, disconcerted. "Good. I will feel immensely better knowing that he is all right."

Sixteen

Back at Haven House, safe in her own room overlooking the confined back garden, sleep did not come easily to Rachel. She twisted and turned under the covers, restless and hot, the room feeling suffocating. She wanted to go outside, wanted to feel the patter of rain that she could hear tapping against her window on her bare skin.

She wanted to be free.

But a well-bred young lady did not wander outside in the middle of the night. It just wasn't done. Of course well bred young ladies did not attend boxing matches where half-naked young men—

She abandoned that disturbing line of thought.

When she finally did sleep, it was an uneasy rest agitated by dreams. She dreamed of home, Haven Court. She flew, oddly at peace, her arms spread and leaning into the wind, above the fells of Yorkshire, swooping like a bird over rounded peaks and down slopes. It was a strange sensation, and yet felt natural and right.

But then the dreams changed. She knew she was unhappy. She longed for something. For someone. What was it? *Who* was it? Amorphous spirits and wild imaginings plagued her, and she awoke often to the sound of the rain, pelting stronger, the wind scraping a branch on her windowpane.

Finally the wind died down and the rain stopped, and despite her restless tossing and turning, she felt herself drift, the precursor to deeper sleep.

And her father came to her, his face seamed with the worry lines that had always, as long as she could remember, dressed his weary face. But he opened his arms and she was a little girl again, running to him in the garden at Haven Court.

And he held her.

"Trust your heart, Rose-red," he murmured, using his pet name for her.

She opened her mouth but her voice was not that of her as a child, but her as a woman. "How, Papa? How do I trust?" She looked into his tired, defeated eyes and experienced a rush of longing so powerful it was like a fist in her stomach. Why had he died and left her alone?

"Let go of worry; let go of fear. Believe in your heart. You will find a way."

Hands grasped her and dragged her away from him. "Papa!" she cried out. She could see blood on his bruised face and she screamed, awakening to the silence of her dim room, her heart pounding, her head aching miserably.

When she lay back down on her pillow, damp from her tears, she still did not know the answer. How did she learn to trust—herself or anyone else?

Morning finally came and found Rachel agitated and restless still, feeling adrift after her

frightening experience of the night before and
the wild dreams that inevitably followed. She
picked at breakfast, never her favorite meal anyway, and her day was brightened only by finding
that her grandmother was much improved in
spirits and health, though still weak and tired.

After that she could settle to nothing, and, after
a miserable walk in the tiny walled garden, the
leaden sky reflecting her grim mood, she returned
to the house. Finally, she paced in the dark hallway
and waited. Would Andromeda remember to tell
Colin to come see her? Would he come?

Details of the dreams of her restless night came
back to haunt her. She had thought at first that
she and her father were in the garden, but it
turned out to be a boxing ring. That explained
the blood on his brow as she was pulled away
from him, she supposed. But she had not been
thinking of her father. Why had he shown up in
her dreams? Why had she not just dreamed of
the fight she had seen?

None of it made any sense.

There was a tap at the door, and Rachel waved
the butler away impatiently, answering it herself.
He would complain in the servant's hall, no doubt,
but she was past caring about such petty concerns.

"Colin, you came!"

She would have reached out to him, so happy
was she to see him upright and conscious, but
there was a stiff look on his face and his jaw was
bruised, a colorful welt marring the clean line.
Dark whiskers sprouted where it was clearly too
painful for his valet to shave.

"Miss Neville. Could we talk someplace private?"

Alerted by his tone and formal manner of addressing her, she calmed herself and escorted him into the parlor, leaving the door ajar. At the far end, a fire was blazing in the grate against the dampness of the day, Rachel supposed, after the steady rain of the night before, but she was too warm already, so instead of the big chairs near the fireplace, she chose a seating group near the window.

"Are you all right?" she asked, examining his face. There was a small cut near his eye, and his lip was split and swollen. Other than that and the bruised jaw, he appeared to be fine. But who knew what bruises he had on other parts of him, parts that could not be seen? She blushed at the direction of her thoughts, and the sight of him in just his breeches intruded again on her wandering wits. She sternly harnessed them in, like wayward ponies, and looked at him expectantly.

"I am just fine." His voice was tight with tension. "How is your grandmother? I hear she has been unwell."

"She is getting better. Yesterday she was up for a while, and today we expect her to join us for luncheon. I saw her just this morning, and she seems to me to be much improved. I would be happy if you would tell your sister that Grandmother thanks her for the jelly, and says it was delicious."

"You may send her a note yourself. I doubt if she will speak to me right now."

"Oh?"

"We had a dustup this morning and have not spoken to each other since."

Rachel frowned at the news. Andromeda and Colin fighting? Though they often sniped at each other, they never fought. She had always thought that beneath the casual affection lay a greater reliance upon each other than even among her own siblings.

"I must say," he continued, "that I was shocked and displeased at your attendance last evening at the fight."

She had expected that, and nodded, about to launch into the set speech she had planned to explain and apologize, but he was not done.

"I am especially shocked," he said, standing and pacing, his homely country jacket flapping about him, "that it was you. You! I always thought you were sensible. Pamela was the one prey to all kinds of freakish behavior and odd starts. And even Andy; I have known her on occasion to do things that are out of the ordinary, to say the least. And Belinda . . . well, we know how wild she is. But you! Sensible, ladylike Rachel, to dress in men's clothes and . . ."

His disgust was so deep he could not find words to express it, it seemed to Rachel. She felt the beginning itch of anger, and could not say it was unwelcome. It was an agreeable alternative to the strange tumultuous longings she had been experiencing. She was about to respond when he planted himself on the carpet in front of her and continued yet again.

"You risked your reputation . . . nay, even your life . . . going to such a place!" His voice vibrated with anger. "How could you do it? How could you justify dressing as a man and venturing out to a boxing match? I am asking you plainly, how do you rationalize such . . . such freakish, ill-timed, ill-considered, wild, unconscionably unnatural . . ."

"Then shut up so I can tell you!"

Colin clamped his mouth shut. He stood, hands clasped behind his back, feet planted apart on the carpet, mouth set in a grim line. "Then tell me," he said, in a resentful tone.

Given the opportunity, Rachel did not know what to say, or even why she should speak at all. She looked up at him, his hard masculinity and angry demeanor a new side to Colin, one she did not at all like to see in her previously indulgent friend and neighbor. He was not her father, nor her brother, nor even her husband that she need justify her behavior to him. Anger flared once again, welcome for the protection from weepiness it offered her. Her whole life since she was a child, since the death of her dear father, had been spent protecting herself: her clothes, her skin, her feelings, her reputation. And what had it gained her? She did not even know herself.

Nor did she trust herself. She overthought every decision and had become narrow in her focus. Which was how she had ended up affianced to Yarnell, an eminently safe, sensible, supremely rational choice as a husband. And all wrong for her. The first right thing she had done in an age was to trust her instincts and free him to be with the woman who loved him, and whom he loved.

"No," she said, with sudden decisiveness. "I am not going to justify or rationalize myself to you or anyone. I am a grown woman. When I marry, I will have to be obedient to my hus . . . though why should I? Am I not capable of making decisions for myself?"

"Evidently not, since you decided to go to a boxing match dressed as a man. Was not that the height of ill thinking?" His tone was of wounded male sensibility.

"We had a very good reason for being there. Andromeda was worried . . ."

"Keep Andy out of this. She will have to answer for her own behavior . . ."

"You impossible, arrogant, idiotic boor!" Rachel stood and faced her angry friend, glaring into his dark eyes. "Andromeda is a grown woman, and her only concern was for your safety. She is your sister and your elder, not your child. I, too, will determine my own path, and you have no right to criticize or . . ."

"I have every right, the right of every proper thinking, intelligent . . ."

"Do not interrupt me again," Rachel said, deadly calm now, "or I will walk out of this room and not come back."

His brows furrowed. "This is not like you, Rachel," he said, his tone wounded. "You have always been so calm and ladylike, so perfectly behaved."

"Yes. And now I have been shrieking like a fish-wife. My perfect behavior made it easier for everyone, didn't it? When I was perfectly be-haved, afraid if I stepped outside the prison walls for one minute everyone would stop approving of me, would stop liking me, would stop *caring*, I made life much easier for everyone else, didn't I? But this is me, Colin. I am as you see me."

"I do not believe you. You aren't one way your whole life and then suddenly overnight change into someone else."

She gave up. How could she explain to him the revolution within her? She squared her shoulders and stiffened her spine. "Colin, I am sorry that my outcry at the fight caused you to lose the bout. I am sincerely sorry, and you can wager it will not happen again. In fact," she continued, resentfully, "if you want to go out and get pummeled and battered every night of your life for the *rest* of your life, then it is all the same to me." She turned and walked to the door, but looked over her shoulder and said, "I trust you can find your own way out. Good day, Colin."

The dowager Lady Haven, who had been sleeping peacefully in a chair by the parlor fire, had awakened as Colin and Rachel's voices raised. She had thought it politic not to alert them to her presence, and besides, she wanted to eavesdrop. It was well worth it.

Rachel had always been her least favorite grandchild. She had considered her spoiled by her great beauty and cold by nature. Not that she had always been like that. As a young girl, Rachel had been sunny and sweet natured, a joy to have around. But at some point she had frozen into the perfectly coiffed, perfectly behaved young lady so approved of in society.

She had been surprised and pleased when she showed the great good sense to jilt that bore, Yarnell. And now, hearing her raise her voice and stand up for herself . . . it did her old heart good and confirmed what she had suspected for some time: beneath her perfect behavior, Rachel was the grandchild most like herself. Within her resided all the instincts of a shrew, and it would take a strong man to stand up to her anger, once unleashed.

But what was between her and Colin? And what was this about Rachel dressing in men's clothes and cavorting with Andromeda Varens and Belinda de Launcey at a boxing match? What a fascinating picture that made. Oh, she could easily picture the gaunt and tall Andromeda Varens pulling off the masquerade, but the exquisitely lovely Miss Rachel Neville? What a pretty fellow she would make.

She snorted with laughter.

"Who's there?"

She had imagined that Colin would have followed Rachel out of the room. Clearly he had not. He had likely stayed behind to brood.

"I said, who is there?"

"Your conscience, lad."

"My lady," he said, with a sigh of resignation and coming around to face her in her deep wing chair. "Why do you always seem to be present for my most humiliating moments?"

"Perhaps because you have so many of them. Though I am surprised you count this among them. I would think you rather proud of yourself: mortally offended manhood, upbraiding a lady who will not toe the line of ladylike, *proper* behavior."

He acknowledged her sarcasm with a grimace. "You do not know what I have been through in the last day."

"No, I don't suppose I do." She looked him over with interest, noting the bruises and cuts, but also the weary resignation on his face. She had once considered him a negligible character, pompous, a bore and a prude. But the last couple of months had proved there was more to Sir Colin Varens than just his rank—a baby baronet, she had always called him—and his stuffy demeanor. "So why don't you tell me what you have been through?"

He slumped into the chair by her and she listened as he related the tale of his boxing career, brief as it had been so far, and the match the night before and how in the middle of a very intense exchange with Sussex Sam, he had heard a voice cry out and had known instantly it was Rachel.

"How did you know?"

He covered his face with his gloveless hands and groaned. "I just knew," he said, taking his hands away and staring at his companion. "I heard her and the fear in her voice, and looked up. I found her, even though she was dressed in hideous male togs. How she expected to pass as a man, I do not know. Really! She is the most beautiful and feminine lady I have ever seen in my life, and no men's clothes and curl-brimmed beaver were going to hide that."

"And yet she passed, apparently, until . . ."

"Until I got hit on the chin. Sam took advantage of my wandering wits and landed me a good one. I fell back, and the next thing I knew, Rachel was bent over me, her gorgeous hair streaming down over her shoulders and . . ."

"What is it?" The dowager leaned forward, examining the young man's face.

His expression was suddenly thoughtful, his brow still furrowed but his gaze unfocused, as if he was looking inward, for a change. "There were

". . . she was . . . she was crying. Her eyes had tears in them."

"Tears? She wept over you, eh?" The dowager said nothing more, but examined his face with interest. Colin Varens had a bony, hard-jawed face, intensely male, vigorously homely. And yet his dark eyes were clear and bright, his hair glossy and curly. His plain visage did not detract from a kind of virile sensuality emanating from him. The dowager imagined that there were likely many women attracted to him who were not quite sure why, given his lack of looks. He had gained, since coming to London, a more self-assured demeanor.

He had been silent for a few moments as he pondered some inner question. He looked up into the dowager's eyes. "Why would any woman come to a boxing match?" he asked, wonder in his voice.

"It sounds as if Rachel and your sister were worried about you. Men die in matches."

"But I won't," he said.

Short sighted and typically male, the dowager thought. There was no arguing with that kind of blind self-assurance, and she was too old a woman even to try. "I wish I had been able to sneak into a match when I was younger. Wouldn't have minded seeing two such muscular specimens battering each other a little." She blatantly looked him over, judging the breadth of his shoulders and thickness of arms. She would have given much to know what Rachel's reaction was on first sight of his body. "No shirt, I'd wager. I wouldn't mind a look at that." She started to laugh when she saw the shock and dismay on his face. "You must learn, Varens, that women are not delicate china figurines to keep on a shelf and take down to examine and dust once every fortnight. Rachel is a woman. Nothing more, nothing less. Remember that."

She felt her eyelids grow heavy and knew that sleep would soon claim her. Sitting upright made sleep easier, since she could not breathe well when prone. But before she slept, she wanted to say one more thing. She had heard, in Rachel's voice, something that led her to believe there was a spark, or perhaps more, of affection for Colin, if he would just treat her well and learn how to fan the flames.

But then, as her eyes drifted closed and Colin took her hand, kissing it as he murmured his good-byes, it occurred to her that if Colin and Rachel were to find each other, it must be with no interference, or no one would ever know if it was love or expediency. They must find their way to each other on their own, if they ever were to do so.

She stayed silent and drifted to sleep, back to the past and dreams of former lovers.

Seventeen

Rachel, sitting in the gloomy drawing room netting a purse for a wedding present for Pamela, looked up as the butler showed a gentleman into the room and stood as Sir Parnell Waterford approached her, hat in hand.

"Miss Neville," he said, bowing over her hand. He waited until the butler exited and said, "I trust you have fully recovered from your experience last night?"

Rachel stiffened. Was he going to take her to task, too? She sat and indicated a chair to the knight. "I am perfectly fine, Sir Parnell. I cannot imagine why anyone would think me injured by the experience."

"Indeed, I expected to find you just as I have, calm and unruffled." He settled himself, adjusting his coattails and planting his booted feet precisely together.

"Thank you, sir. It is gratifying to meet *one* gentleman who does not think I am some precious featherbrain who must be wrapped in cotton wadding." She picked up her netting again.

"I take it Colin has been to see you?"

"He has." She wadded her netting work into a messy bundle and tossed it away from her, trying to conceal her agitation. She was afraid she was not doing a very good job.

"In his defense, he is very old fashioned. I doubt if he has ever heard of, much less read, *A Vindication of the Rights of Woman.*"

Rachel regarded the man sitting before her closely. She had assumed he would be the usual, in her admittedly limited experience, run of self-made men, shrewd rather than clever and narrow in his beliefs and thoughts. That he should be more liberal in his views should teach her never to prejudge a person based on social status or trade. "That does not excuse his behavior. Nor have I ever read . . . whatever you just mentioned, but I would never accuse someone of . . ." She broke off, anger rising in her again like a full moon tide.

"Of?" His graying eyebrows lifted.

She took a deep breath. "He berated me in my own home with . . . what did he say? Being freak-ish, wild, unnatural . . . and said he expected better of me."

"I assume, then, that this behavior—going to a boxing match dressed as a man—is not something you would, in the normal course of things, do."

"No," she admitted. "I have always been the well-behaved one in our family. It is much more like my younger sister, Pamela, to have larks." Rachel pensively examined her outstretched right hand, her baby finger adorned with the amber ring her fa-ther had given her on her twelfth birthday, the year before he died. "But why must I always be so? Will no one love me anymore if I decide to *do* something for once in my life? When Andromeda asked me to go with her . . ."

"This was Miss Varens's idea?"

His hasty utterance made her look up at him. He was sitting on the edge of his seat, turning his hat around and around in his hands.

"Yes," she said, hoping she was not revealing something she should not have.

But the knight did not look perturbed. On the contrary, he looked . . . invigorated, stimulated. He was trying to conceal a smile.

"She is worried about Colin and said that every good general knew one must study the enemy to defeat it. She is determined to stop your practice of the sport, and condemns pugilism as brutal and inhuman."

The knight looked thoughtful. The smile lingered on his lips, and he shook his head. "I should have known Miss Varens was behind this. She has been a most vocal opponent to my training of her brother." He stood and bowed. "I will not keep you longer, Miss Neville. My purpose was to make sure you had taken no harm—no physical harm—from last night's set-to, but I can see from your blooming health that you have recovered nicely. Will we be seeing you at another fight?"

"No," Rachel said, standing as well. "I do not care a jot what happens to Colin in the ring, and you may tell him so when next you see him."

"I shall certainly tell him that he is being an idiot," Sir Parnell said, with a comic wink.

Rachel, not certain how to interpret his words, replied, "Thank you, sir. Good day."

Andromeda Varens sat at a round table by the window in the stately drawing room of the Strongwycke city manor, and stared out the window, thinking ruefully of all that Belinda could tell her uncle if she chose. It would be a lengthy letter, and shocking to the reader, no doubt. She imagined Belinda's letter saying:

Dear Uncle,
Great fun! Since I have been staying with Miss Varens, I have been groped shockingly by a dirty stranger in a theater pit seat, only barely escaped a riot in that same theater, and saw a bully box-ing match while dressed as a boy. I only just escaped with my disguise intact. What larks! You were perfectly right to entrust me to such a staid and reliable lady. Hope to see you soon, etc.

She leaned her elbows on the table and put her face in her hands. Colin had been absolutely right. She had been a complete fool to take Be-linda into that atmosphere, though the girl was perfectly fine after their night out, and indeed claimed to have enjoyed the experience. From now on, it would be only the safest of venues for Belinda.

She should have gone alone. That was her great sin, talking Rachel into accompanying her and taking Belinda with them. She should have instead left the child with Rachel and gone alone. If there ever was a next time, that was what she would do.

The stiff and proper Strongwycke butler, who always made her feel faintly as if she was in the wrong with her country manners—she had al-ways prided herself on her exquisite refinement, but things had changed since twelve years before, her come-out year, and she was not at all *au courant* or even *comme il faut*—entered, bowed, and announced, in funereal tones, "Sir Parnell Waterford."

"Oh, Larkson, tell him I am not home," she said, starting up from her chair. "Or let me . . ."

"You could tell me that yourself, Miss Varens," Sir Parnell said, following the butler closely. "Or I will avert my eyes and you may make your escape undetected. I will then leave a message that I hope the lady suffered no ill effects from the shocking conclusion to the night, and that she has my unbounded admiration for daring what so few ladies would, for the sake of her brother."

"Are you being facetious, sir?" she asked, sharply, glaring up at him as she sank back down into her chair.

"No. Not at all."

He strolled in, turning his hat around and around in his hands. As always, he was exquisitely dressed. Colin should go to his tailor, if he could afford him, Andromeda thought. She watched the gentleman, troubled, wondering why she could not view him as the enemy, when surely she should. But he had been so kind to her. And he was so very interesting. As much as she had tried to dislike him, she found she really could not.

"But I would like to make you an offer . . . a wager, if you will."

She had not invited him to sit, but he took a chair opposite hers at the round table.

Cautiously, she said, "And what might the wager be, sir?"

"I would like you to learn what your brother has learned, to see the science behind what might look, to the untrained eye, to be savagery."

Taken aback, Andromeda shook her head before she had even thought it through.

"Think about it," he said. "Do not just dismiss it out of hand." The knight leaned over, stared directly into her eyes, and said, "You said that one must know the enemy. Well, if pugilism is the enemy, I dare you to try it. To learn about it. If you do, and still consider it mere barbarism, then I will try to talk Colin out of boxing. Only try, mind, because I think it beyond my powers. But I pledge to you that I will make a concerted effort, if you just take the chance and learn more about it."

"Then I will," she said, stung by his smile into replying immediately. "Where and when?"

"Here. Tomorrow morning. I happen to know that your brother has an appointment tomorrow morning that will keep him for most of the hours between ten and one, and then he has a luncheon engagement with a friend. I have scheduled another fight for him tomorrow evening. I would not have him lose his nerve after last night's unfortunate rout, though I do not think that likely to happen with so fierce a warrior as your brother. So shall we say tomorrow morning at ten-thirty? Miss de Launcey may act as your second, for propriety's sake."

"For propriety . . ." She shook her head. "I have gone so far beyond propriety lately that I do not know why anyone would even worry about it in relation to me."

"Nevertheless, I would not have you be the object of gossip among his lordship's staff unnecessarily. Is it agreed?"

"It is," she said, taking his outstretched hand.

Neither of them wore gloves, and his hand was warm and dry, his grip firm. What had she just gotten herself into?

Colin, dressed for his fight in just his breeches—no shirt was worn so no loose clothing could hinder the fighter—listened to last minute instructions from Sir Parnell. The room was just as it had been two nights before, though warmer and even smokier.

"This fellow is called Bristol Bob. He's a bruiser, Colin, and will go for your stomach. He's known for very punishing blows. Go for his chest, for he is often short of wind and you can get the advantage of him that way."

"I don't need the advantage. I will beat him man to man, whatever way he wants to fight." He knew his tone was grim, but he didn't care.

"Colin," Parnell said, grabbing his shoulders.

"What is it?"

"You are fit to fight, are you not?"

"Never felt better."

"I mean mentally, not physically. You are not brooding over anything, are you?"

Like the fact that the woman he loved was making a blasted idiot of herself by attending a boxing match, for God's sake? He didn't say it, but felt the anger burn in his gut again. What was wrong with her? Why was she acting so differently, when she had never before—

"Colin!"

"What?"

"You have not been attending again. Your opponent has just stepped onto the floor." The knight shook him by the shoulders and stared into his eyes. "Colin, if I am not convinced you are ready for this, by God I will pull you out. I swear it. I will end the fight."

Taking in a deep breath, Colin straightened and focused on his opponent. He was a thickset fellow, younger than Colin by several years, but likely more experienced in the ways of London fights. Parnell was right. He must focus, or he would be beaten. He glanced around, and he could see that the bettors were taking Bristol Bob to win. No doubt they had all been there two nights before to see Colin beaten by Sussex Sam.

Well, he would show them. There would be no repetition of that humiliation. This was the one thing, apart from farming, that he was good at, and no one was going to beat him without a damned good fight.

He stepped up to the chalk mark and took his position, glaring deep into his opponent's eyes. This he could do. He might be a damned poor man for the ladies, he might never be more than a buffoon on the ballroom dance floor, but *this* he could do.

It was over in minutes, and he was the victor. He took grim satisfaction in the look of surprise on many of the spectators' faces as he stood over the prone body of his opponent. No man would doubt his abilities again.

June drifted on, wending its way inevitably toward its end. The Haven family party would have already left London but for Grand's illness; they must wait until she was well enough to travel, so they remained. Rachel rather wished for an end to the Season instead of this dwindling, fading movement toward the heat of a city summer. She had never been in London for so long, and she found that though there was much to do, one did reach an end to enjoyment of balls and musicales and Venetian breakfasts.

Colin, Andromeda, and Belinda were kind enough to remain, though, bearing them company until nearly the time when they would leave. Rachel found that though with the exodus of many of the better families to the country her invitations to the ubiquitous balls and routs were more sparse, they were replaced by interesting things to do, places she had never been, sights she had never seen. There were literary afternoons and a bird-watching expedition with Andromeda's eclectic group of friends, met in her wandering; though Rachel was not terribly interested in birds, it was a joy for the country air, and a lovely respite from London. And there were city joys to take part in, too: A boat trip on the Thames that, while odorous, was at least interesting in its scenic diversity. Chelsea, especially, viewed from the river was fascinating.

And one memorable day she, Andromeda, and Belinda went to see a balloon elevation. The dashing French pilot invited her to climb in and enjoy a tethered ride. Belinda came with her, but Andromeda resolutely refused, saying that heights made her uncomfortable.

It was thrilling, the feeling of going up causing an odd fluttering in her stomach like the flight of a hundred butterflies. The pilot, gallant and courteous though he was, had pressed himself a little too close, but did not take other liberties. Belinda, her brown eyes shining, was enraptured by the experience and begged to accept the pilot's invitation to go for a real balloon ride, but that Rachel and Andromeda would not allow.

And yet all the while, Rachel was aware of a frisson of unhappiness behind it all. She could not be comfortable while she and Colin were on such bad terms, especially since she must see him often. Why it bothered her she was not sure; he had been abominably managing, and she would not climb back into the velvet-lined box from which she had escaped.

But at last, as June reached its midpoint, it would soon be time to go back to Yorkshire. Grand was recovering apace. She and Rachel's mother had made a strange kind of peace and were even undertaking the redecoration of Haven House together. It was all a jumble of wall coverings, bolts of fabric, and splashes of paint, and new furniture would appear and disappear on a daily basis.

It was a good time to be out of the house, and the weather was agreeable, so Rachel welcomed a proposed day trip to an estate that Sir Parnell was considering purchasing, even though it would necessitate spending more time in Colin's company than she was comfortable with. It was strange: they were at odds, and yet she had never been more aware of him than she now was. She told herself time and again to just ignore him, but it would not do. Inevitably he would take her arm to help her over a rough spot or a step, and her elbow would tingle from the contact. Or their eyes would meet, and she would find it impossible to just look away.

He was a dark-eyed, silent stranger now, where in past he had always been smiling, always obsequious. Now he watched her, but it was with a serious expression, not the moony, calf-love look she had come to know and despise. And with his regard came a nervous twitch in her belly and an odd yearning for more of his touch, just that hand on her elbow or the brush of his fingertips.

She resigned herself to more of that same awareness—what could not be explained must be ignored—and readied for the journey with some excitement, wearing her favorite rose striped carriage dress and a new bonnet, bought for a fetching display of ripe cherries that nodded cunningly over the brim. She took great pains with her hair and every other detail of her appearance.

She had a feeling about this day, that it would prove to be a day of revelations. Reflecting on it later, she realized that she had been right, but not in any way she could have foreseen.

It was a gorgeous mid-June day, with mare's tail clouds high in the azure sky. The ride in the Strongwycke carriage was surprisingly comfortable, the roads dry and reasonably smooth. Colin and Sir Parnell rode their horses while the ladies traveled in the open carriage, their journey lasting only an hour, with no need for any stops along the way, and conversation flowed. Belinda was becoming more knowledgeable about the countryside under Andromeda's expert tutelage, and joyed in pointing out larkspur and juniper, alder and hawthorn stands. The estate was a

pretty gray stone house set on a hillside and looking over an ornamental pond. Though the
gardens were neglected, thickly overgrown with
wild roses and briars, they showed great promise.
Andromeda and Sir Parnell, walking arm in arm,
exclaimed over every detail, from the dovecote to
the immaculate stables, but especially the house.

There was still a housekeeper resident, though
the former owner had died two years before, and
she was able to tell them much about the estate
and its history. Sir Parnell already knew much
about the estate because the current owner was a
planter in the Caribbean, a friend of his for many
years, and had often told the knight tales of the
house. As the fellow never intended to come
back to England, he was willing to sell it at a rea-
sonable price just to be clear of its upkeep, which
was draining his purse with no return, as he did
not like to rent it.

Rachel, still not talking to Colin, strolled arm
in arm with Belinda, while Colin shot her earnest
looks. She had the sense that he wished to speak
to her, but she was not sure she wanted to talk to
him. Life had changed. *She* had changed. What
was there to speak of?

They went inside to a cold luncheon, followed
by dessert out on the terrace. As the housekeeper
set out a dish of late strawberries culled from the
shady bramble-covered gardens of the estate, Sir
Parnell invited Andromeda to walk in the garden
with him, and Rachel noticed Belinda hugging
herself with excitement.

"You are almost floating off your chair, Belinda.
What has got you so happy?"

"I know a secret!" she said, brown eyes shining.

"You will never keep a secret if you taunt others with it," Colin said, with a smile. He dipped a strawberry in sugar and clotted cream and was about to pop it into his mouth, but instead offered it to Rachel, with a lift of his eyebrows.

"A peace offering?" she murmured, accepting it from him, her lips closing around the tips of his naked fingers as she took the succulent berry. If he was willing to grovel a little, she might consider accepting his apology.

"Consider it what you will," he said, coolly.

She gave him a challenging look. So, no apology, though he was making peace in his own way. Not the Colin of previous years, then, who would prostrate himself before her to beg for her favor. She rather liked the new Colin, oddly. He was more of a man for refusing to be subjugated.

She noticed that he watched while she ate it, though, despite his casual tone. She became preternaturally aware of every one of her actions, even down to licking her cream-smeared lips. He looked away with a tight frown on his face and swallowed hard, squinting into the distance. *Now* what was wrong with him? He was unfathomable.

Rachel turned back to Belinda, who was watching them both with a peculiar look of disgust. "What is your secret?" Rachel asked, dismissing Colin's odd behavior.

"It is not a secret if I tell anyone else. And I don't know for sure. It's just something I've guessed."

"That isn't a secret then," Colin said. "A guess is not a secret."

They bickered like siblings while Rachel watched Andromeda and Sir Parnell, alerted that something unusual was happening by their stance, closer than necessary, and their stillness. If she did not know better . . .

Sir Parnell was looking down at her with his hands on her shoulders and she was gazing steadily up at him, her hat off and hanging down her back by the ribbon. And then, extraordinarily, he kissed her, just once and briefly, but definitely on the lips. Rachel glanced over at Belinda, her mouth open to exclaim at such odd behavior, but she saw the look of knowing exultation on the girl's face.

"Do you think . . ."

Belinda nodded, her smile breaking into a broad grin.

"Really?" Rachel gasped. "How did this come about?"

Colin looked from one to the other with a frown. "What are you two talking about?"

"If you can't guess, then I shan't tell you," Belinda said, with a saucy bob of her head. She turned back to Rachel. "Well, you see, Sir Parnell has been over a lot lately, teaching . . ." She glanced over at Colin, then moved closer to Rachel and whispered, "Teaching Miss Varens to box!"

"Really?" Rachel was stunned, and puzzled that Andromeda had kept the lessons a secret.

"Yes! It was wonderfully funny at first, you know, for Miss Varens would dress in breeches and square off with Sir Parnell. But he taught her everything, and she has gotten quite good at it. Have you not noticed lately that she no longer talks of making Sir Colin stop?"

"That is true. Why?"

"She said the other day that it truly is a science. If you learn how to box properly, then you need never fear being hurt, because you know how to be hit."

Rachel shook her head. "That sounds very unlike Andromeda."

Belinda shrugged.

"But how did *this* start?" Rachel asked, indicating with a nod of her head the couple, now strolling back toward the terrace.

"I was there every day, for Sir Parnell insisted I be propriety, as he called me. After the lesson, he would stay for luncheon sometimes, or they would talk. And when we have all gone out, they are together almost always. Have you not noticed?"

"How blind I have been! Now that you say it, I can see it, but I never would have suspected otherwise. How self-centered I have been!" Wistfully watching the couple approach, she saw a radiance on Andromeda's handsome face and a quiet satisfaction on the knight's. "How wonderful this is for them both. It could not have happened to two more deserving people. And this, I would imagine, is why he is now thinking of buying an estate when he has been hitherto perfectly comfortable in his London rooms."

Belinda nodded. "Isn't it wonderful? I like him. He is a very clever gentleman. He used to own slaves, you know, and he told me all about life in the Caribbean. He is now an anti-slaver and has come to London to try to end the practice. He told Andromeda a shocking story one day about a man who used to beat his poor slaves, and how it made him sick to his heart." She frowned thoughtfully. "I think that is when Andromeda really knew how she felt about him, for he was so horrified, and you could see in his eyes how de-

termined he is to change things. She just stared
and stared at him, and he stared back. I felt like
I should slink away, they gazed into each other's
eyes so long."

"I have never heard before of such an odd woo-
ing, to be sure," Rachel said. "Boxing lessons and
reform talk. He shall set a precedent among the
gentlemen."

"What *are* you two talking about?" Colin asked,
finally mystified beyond endurance.

"We are speaking," Belinda said archly. "About
the likelihood that . . ."

"We are getting married," Andromeda said,
beaming, held close in Sir Parnell's arms as they
made it to the terrace and joined the company.
"We are getting married and we will live here."

Eighteen

Rachel and Belinda leaped up to congratulate the couple, hugging them both in an extravagant display of emotion. But Colin sat staring off over the gentle decline toward the garden, misty in the midday heat of the English countryside. He could not quite take it all in. In one moment, every element of his life had changed.

"Colin, are you not happy for me?" Andromeda said.

"Of course I am," he said, rising and holding out his hand to his friend, Sir Parnell. He glanced from one to the other, the handsome though brown knight and the woman who would never look like a blooming twenty year old again, his beloved sister. Almost his conscience, he would have said. "I am happy for you, if this is what you really want. But you need not marry, you know. I only joke about your being an old maid. I never meant it."

"But I *want* to marry," Andromeda said, coloring.

He heard the hurt in her voice and stood, approaching her. Damn his clumsiness anyway! He would not injure her feelings for anything. "Then I am happy for you." He hugged his sister.

In truth, he was shaken, this one event rocking his world more than he would ever admit to anyone. It had never occurred to him that Andromeda would marry. When he had imagined, in years gone by, marrying Rachel and taking her to Corleigh, it was always knowing in the background that Andromeda would stay, keep house for them, and Rachel would not need to care for all the petty details of running an estate. He had wanted her to be able just to sit in the parlor, embroider or net, and go for the occasional walk with him. He and Andromeda would take care of all the mundane details of life so Rachel could just concentrate all her efforts on staying the perfectly lovely, perfectly delicate English rose she was.

This day had changed many things, and made him wonder about many more. Was no one whom he had thought? Was he doomed to find, though his life, that his judgments had been pretty far from reality all through the years? Pamela, little imp-wanderer and eternally youthful boyish girl-child, had captured and married the sophisticated, intelligent Earl of Strongwycke. Rachel—the cool, pragmatic, icy calm beauty expected to marry well—had rejected an eligible marquess for no good reason that anyone could imagine, except that she did not love him and he did not love her.

And Andromeda, devoted sister, lifelong spinster, was engaged to marry a Caribbean nabob.

As they returned home, he let his horse take him far ahead of the others, needing some time to adjust to the changes in his life. No Rachel, ever. That was the hardest thing, and perhaps he had only just accepted it, finally and for good. Watching her eat the cream-dipped strawberry, he had felt that old rush of physical longing that was more than mere sexual desire. It radiated from some core of him that was so saturated with Rachel that her name was engraved on his heart. As much as he tried to eradicate it, it would not go away.

He was in love with her. Even this new Rachel, the one who had adventures and rode in hot air balloons and acted the hoyden on occasion. He still loved her. It should have given him a disgust of her. It truly should have been what erased his emotional attachment to her once and for all, for she had exceeded the boundaries of what he had always thought of as ladylike. She was not the Rachel he had fallen in love with.

Or was she?

She was still as lovely as ever, but her beauty was only a small part of what he had always believed he had loved about her.

He still saw her in pensive moments. There was a vulnerability in her that he had sensed from a very young age. It had attracted him, had created within him his powerful urge to shelter and protect her. She had, since her father died, cloaked her emotions within a hard shell, turning away any tender sentiment. But he had felt her pain and shared it, remembering how it hurt to lose his mother when he was about the same age. And he had wanted to protect her from any more pain in her life, however unrealistic that had been. He wanted to be her guardian, her valiant knight protector.

Now she was coming out of that shell, and he had seen how her vivacity and new liveliness had attracted a different sort of man than had courted her in past. Yarnell had thought she would be a doll to put up on a shelf and admire: perfectly gowned and coiffed, perfectly lovely, and perfectly cold. But hadn't he been treating her much the same as the despised marquess? Hadn't that very expectation, that he could keep her cloistered and protected, leaving to Andromeda all the real work of running an estate, been an insult to her strength and independence?

She had been right to tell Yarnell to release her, and she had been right to say no to his own proposals all those years. Whatever her reasons had been, she had been absolutely right. There was more to her than the brittle, beautiful shell. She was emerging like a butterfly from a chrysalis, to use a hoary old metaphor for a lady of her loveliness. She was shedding her fears, leaving behind her vulnerability, showing her strength of character, and yet he could not cast off his emotions for her as easily.

She was still precious to him, and he still wanted her in every way a man could want a woman.

So he truly did love her, bone deep. He had thought at first the new Rachel would not appeal to him, but he had been wrong. He longed for her even more, humbled by her strength, attracted by her new boldness in a way he never would have believed. And yet he knew his chances to attach her were just as remote, or perhaps more so, especially with the grim way he had been treating her lately, stubborn boor that he was. Many men would seek her out. One of them would surely capture her heart, for he instinctively knew that with the changes in her there would be a warming of the frost that had encapsulated her for so many years. And some lucky man would find a way to turn that flicker of warmth into fire.

With that glum thought, he came to the London turnoff and waited for the carriage and Sir Parnell. He must concentrate on his sister's marriage. He owed her much for years of patience and companionship, love and nurturing. Without even thinking about it, he knew they would be happy. It had only ever needed a man who could appreciate the unique woman she was, and he could not have hoped for a better brother than Sir Parnell Waterford.

Tamping down his own unutterable sadness and plastering a fraudulent smile on his face, he called out, "I propose that we stop at the White Hart and send the innkeeper out for the best bottle of champagne he can find. We have something truly wonderful to celebrate in the marriage of my sister to a man who almost deserves her."

He was rewarded for his effort with a radiant smile from his sister, who had needed only his blessing, he realized, to make her completely happy. They had only two weeks left in London before they must go north, returning Belinda to her uncle and new aunt. He suddenly realized that the trip home would likely be made without his sister, who would be preparing to marry, or perhaps be already married. He must make the most of the next two weeks, for he doubted he would be back down to London any time soon.

As they entered the tavern and he stepped back to allow Rachel and Belinda to advance ahead of him, he decided that he would stop letting his expectations rule him, and would just let each day come and go. It was the only thing he could do.

But that was easier to think than to do. He had to be grateful that he had his fighting. Bouts were scheduled every couple of days, and he won consistently. Pugilism was not without its danger, and he still suffered his share of bruises, scrapes, and cuts, but it felt good to do what he was so very proficient at. Even with Sir Parnell more busy now, a newly engaged man, Colin still found he was learning all the time and getting better. He had attained a reputation, and crowds came to watch him box. He even beat Sussex Sam handily, sending the giant down in just three minutes. That was his most satisfying triumph.

He even wished Rachel could have seen it.

Socially he was finding himself more in demand than he ever would have imagined. Lord and Lady Sommer, a couple Colin had met briefly at a picnic, were holding a ball to honor the first day of the Season so close to their own name. Colin was surprised to find an invitation for himself and Andromeda in the morning mail, since the earl and countess had rather snubbed him when they were introduced. He could only assume that good company was getting very sparse, and he had been moved up to 'acceptable' as a result. It did not hurt, he supposed, that Lord Sommer had bet a very large amount in a fight, backing him, and had won his bet.

It did not surprise him to find that Rachel would be there. Events were infrequent now as most of the better families had left town, and she was everywhere he turned, her radiance always before him, his heart always thrumming painfully at the sight of her.

It was still unfashionably light when he arrived, but he found that he was not the first, as he had feared he would be. He was greeted politely by his host and hostess and made Andromeda's apologies, then wandered for a while, talking to people he had met recently, but more often strolling alone.

When Rachel arrived, he knew it instantly. Every man in the ballroom, it seemed to him, gazed at her with longing. Several were openly courting her, but elusive as she had become, there was no rumor as to which she would choose. It seemed that despite her fears, she had been forgiven by society for jilting Lord Yarnell, even in the face of his mother's determined spite. The dowager Lady Yarnell had removed to Wight for the summer, it was said, to lick her wounds and send plaintive—and, it was rumored, ignored—missives to her hitherto obedient son, who was traveling happily with his unsuitable bride.

Colin was happy Rachel had not been made to suffer for doing the right thing. It could likely be attributed to her beauty, social standing, and the ardor of many more suitors, he supposed, with a cynicism born of a new understanding of London Society. She was a valuable commodity: beautiful, rich, well-born, and with a spotless reputation. As such, she would not be censured when there were likely many matchmaking mothers looking for well-dowered and well-born young ladies for their sons.

He watched as gentlemen flocked to her side. He recognized one or two fortune hunters, some who would gather around any recognized fashionable beauty, but many genuine admirers, all of them much more eligible than he.

She was accompanied by her mother, but that woman looked peevish and ill-tempered and retreated immediately to the chaperones' chairs to gossip with her cronies. As the music started, Rachel's card was no doubt filling with waltzes and galops, mazurkas and country dances.

She looked up and caught his eyes on her. Since his sister's engagement, they had made an uneasy peace, uneasy because it was wretchedly uncomfortable longing for her every waking minute and knowing all hope was dead. She raised the dance card and tiny pencil in pantomime, and he nodded. Yes, he hoped she would put him down for a dance. It would be her decision which one, though he might have to take whatever had not yet been claimed.

Later, about the third or fourth dance, he found that he was right; it was a staid minuet, and they were apart much more than they were together. He supposed he should consider himself lucky it was not one of the more modern dances, for he was not the best on the floor.

"When do you go back north?" he said, as they promenaded at the end of their dance.

"In two weeks. We would have been gone already, but Grandmother is still not fit to travel."

"She seemed much better the last time I saw her," he said, remembering their conversation. She had told him that women were not china figurines to be kept on a shelf. At the time he had brushed aside her remarks as irrelevant to him. Only later had he understood the justice of her accusations. He would have stifled the vibrant woman on his arm with his overcare.

"She is better, but still weak. We will have to take the trip home in easy stages. Haven and Jane are coming down to accompany us home to Yorkshire."

He had been about to offer his own escort as far as their path lay together, but even that was not necessary. He could leave any time, he supposed. "Home to Yorkshire," he murmured.

"I . . . I was thinking of going to visit Pamela for a while. I miss her so much. I never knew how much until recently."

"That would be good for both of you. I'm sure she misses you just as much."

Their desultory conversation was over as her next dance partner came to claim her for the coveted waltz, and he watched them glide across the floor in elegant swooping motions. She must think him a dull dog compared to these London dandies who were all mad for her. She must laugh to herself about old Colin, forever proposing, faithful old dog that he was.

He shrugged and turned, walking away.

Rachel, nominally dancing with Lord Featherfew, was thinking ahead to her return to Yorkshire. What would Colin do, alone at Corleigh? She caught a glimpse of him, and noticed three young ladies had clustered around him, one with her hand daringly on his upper arm. If he wanted, he need not be alone. Many girls would consider themselves lucky to marry him, and knowing him as she did, she knew they would have every chance at a happy marriage. He could be stuffy and hidebound, but he was also kindhearted and good. And he certainly had a vigorous male attractiveness to him, despite his rather homely appearance. Even ladies not in need of a husband had found him attractive.

His new reputation as a winning boxer intrigued many of the ladies. Rachel had heard it whispered among some of the women, ladies who were not supposed to know about such brutal things but clearly did. As for herself, she supposed it was just the shock of the sight, but she could not rid herself of the image of him stripped to the waist, his skin pale as marble, muscles gleaming with sweat, as he fought Sussex Sam. The image taunted her. He had apparently been fighting for years, and yet she had never known of that side of his life. What else about him did she not know? What other layers were there to her old friend, things he had hidden for fear of shocking the delicate flower he had always considered her?

When she was younger, she had treated him as one would a pet puppy, tolerating his eager attentions, rebuffing him when she became bored. And he had thought of her, it seemed, as a hothouse flower, apt to wilt at the slightest breeze. Had he changed most, or had she? Or was it only their images of each other that had changed?

He certainly did not seem like a puppy anymore.

The dance finally ended, and her escort walked with her around the perimeter of the ballroom. Her next dance was not engaged, so she requested they return to her mother.

Instead, her escort suggested, "Will you walk with me in the garden, Miss Neville?"

"That would be lovely, my lord," she said. The ballroom was overheated, and a breath of cooler air was the cure.

They strolled out to the terrace. Lord Featherfew had a rakish reputation, but he was reportedly on the hunt for a wife and had calmed his wilder tendencies. He had given her a fair amount of attention of late, and though he was a pleasant enough fellow, she was not seriously considering him a suitor. In truth, she was not considering anyone a suitor. She was too confused about her own feelings for that.

"That grassy stretch looks cooler, does it not, Miss Neville?"

The lawn wove in and out of ornamental fruit trees and burgeoning gardens of hydrangea and unnamable shrubs. The path beckoned. Cool fingers of shadowy twilight had already tempted another couple, who strolled among the trees.

"It does. Shall we walk there?"

He was an undemanding escort. He was not one for conversation, and she found his company peaceful, rather like being alone. She wondered, as they strolled, should she be considering Colin in the new light shed on his life? Should she be thinking of *him* as a possible husband? That was ridiculous, of course, for he had finally accepted that she would never marry him, and truly seemed happy about it now. That stung, she had to admit to herself. He had been her devoted admirer for so long, she felt adrift without that in the background of her life. At the time she had truly wanted him to leave her alone, but it felt odd now that he had taken her at her word.

"Where are we going, my lord?" she asked, suddenly realizing they were quite alone among the shrubbery and it was darker than she had expected.

"Miss Neville, my dear, you have my most fervent admiration," he said, pulling her around to face him and clutching her against him. "It cannot have escaped your attention that I am your most devoted admirer, and now I wish to prove to you the passion of my attachment."

"Sir, I . . ."

But her words of denial were cut off as he gripped her in an iron grasp and kissed her, hard, his brandy-scented breath mingling with hers as he sucked on her lip and jammed his tongue in her mouth. She gagged and struggled, but he was strong and had her one arm almost bent behind her.

She wrenched her head to the side and cried out, "Stop, my lord, leave me . . ."

He had pulled her close again and found her mouth, smothering it with his own.

But then suddenly he was pulled away from her and as quickly as that happened, he was on the ground, his hand on his jaw. Colin stood over him, fists clenched.

"Leave now, Featherfew, and if you ever come near Miss Neville again, I will kill you, I swear it." Varens's reputation as a fighter had become legend in recent weeks. He had never been beaten since his first abortive battle with Sussex Sam. It was well known that in the rematch Colin had beaten him handily and the fellow had since retired.

The viscount scrambled to his feet and said, "I did not harm her, Varens. Ask her yourself. She let me lead her away from the lighted paths. What else was I to think but that she'd welcome my attentions?"

"She doesn't."

"How do you know?" The fellow, a hurt expression on his handsome face, turned to Rachel. "Miss Neville, I . . ."

"Lord Featherfew," she said, her voice trembling. "You have mistaken my feelings. I did not realize we had strayed so far from the lighted path, or I would not have . . ."

"You don't need to apologize to this lout, Rachel," Colin growled. "Leave, Featherfew." He moved menacingly toward him.

"I most certainly will. I have never been so insulted in all my life!" The viscount, still nursing his jaw, which would likely sport a colorful bruise the next day, strode away, muttering angrily under his breath.

"He has a point, Colin," Rachel said, trying to conceal a smile. Her hero. Rescuing her again, just as he did when she was eight and he thirteen and she had strayed too far from Haven Court and fallen in a pond.

"The important thing is, are you all right, Rachel?" He came to her and put his hands on her shoulders, pulling her gauzy cap sleeves back into place.

"I am. He frightened me, but in retrospect, I can see he thought I would welcome his kisses. I just had been daydreaming and had not realized how far we had strayed." She could not exactly say she had been daydreaming about him.

His expression serious, he said, "You must be careful, Rach. You are so beautiful. More than one man could be tempted to hope you would favor him."

"My beauty does not excuse his behavior," she said, stung by the implication that she was somehow responsible for Featherfew's misbehavior.

"Of course not; I did not mean that. But you are so lovely . . ." He let the sentence hang and there was silence between them.

Then the extraordinary happened.

His expression softened, and his dark eyes blazed like coal. He surrounded her with his arms and pulled her close, hesitated for just a moment, and then kissed her, not hard. Gently he moved, exploring her lips with his.

Nineteen

When the kiss ended, they stared at each other in the dim light from the house and well-lit terrace.

"What . . ." Rachel didn't quite know what to say. It had not been a deep kiss, and certainly not as invasive as Lord Featherfew's, but it had shaken her composure, and she had always prided herself on being imperturbable. She had felt for those few moments as if the simple act of their lips touching was speaking louder than all the words in the world ever could. It had been eloquent, the communication. But what had it meant?

"I'll take you back to the ball. I hope no one has noted our absence."

It was said grimly, and as Colin turned her and marched her back up to the terrace, his grip was unnecessarily hard. She had to trot to keep up to his stride, but once to the terrace she tore her arm from his grasp and said, "I am quite capable of walking on my own without you pulling me along as if I were two years old."

"You certainly were able to walk on your own with that cad, Featherfew," he retorted, turning and staring down at her with an unfathomable expression in his dark eyes.

"He did nothing more than you did!" Her retort rang out in the night air and hung between them, almost visible. She could not believe what she was doing, griping at Colin as if he were Haven.

Though he did not seem anything like a brother in that moment, she thought, with the memory of his kiss on her lips, the feel of his strong hands at her waist. But what did those few seconds in his arms mean set against their long friendship and occasional enmity? She stared steadily at him in the gloom. If only he would help her understand, but he was silent.

She sighed in exasperation, wondering not just what had gotten into him, but also what had gotten into her. Her thoughts tumbled around her head like a swarm of restive kittens. Was the kiss impulse only? Did she enjoy it or hate it? It was not distasteful, like Featherfew's, but she may merely have been shocked into compliance when his lips met hers. She would need to experience the kiss again to know what her true feelings were. Yes, that was definitely the answer. They should kiss again.

Boldly, she said, "Colin, perhaps we should . . ."

"Go inside; I know," he said, averting his gaze from her. He took her arm in a more relaxed grip and strolled with her through the terrace doors as if they had just had a lovely ramble in the safety of the lighted veranda.

There was no further opportunity to talk as her mother, who had been searching for her, was ready to leave, having come down with a convenient headache—convenient because a woman had just arrived whom Lady Haven could not abide.

In the darkness of her bedroom, in the gloom of the night by the guttering light of a single candle, Rachel sat up in her bed rubbing lanolin cream into her elbows as she thought back over the kiss. Why had he kissed her? Men surely did not do anything so absurd as kiss a lady merely out of frustration or pique. Pamela had asked her once what it meant when a gentleman kissed one and one felt tingly all over. Shocked by the question and what it implied about her sister's actions, Rachel had sidestepped the query and berated her about kissing and what it could do to her reputation if she was seen.

But what *did* it mean when a gentleman kissed one and one felt all tingly inside? And why did gentlemen kiss ladies? Silly questions, she supposed, but she had no inkling whether kissing always meant a preference, or if sometimes it could mean something entirely different. Men were so unfathomable, and she had little experience trying to figure them out. There had seemed little point in trying to understand them, for in her admittedly limited experience, understanding them could not aid in attaining a better husband or a more advantageous match, and that was all that had concerned her about gentlemen until this spring.

There was only one way to find out the answer, and that was to ask Colin why he did what he did. Would he answer? She would just force him to, corner him and leave him with no alternative. She would do that the next morning. She closed the glass pot of cream, set it on her bedside table, and snuffed the flickering candle that had almost burned out. But as she lay her head down on her pillow, careful not to disarrange the pomaded curls her maid had pinned into place for the night, she could think of no explanation that would account for that kiss—nor her own tumultuous response to it.

It was quite correct to visit Colin at the Strongwycke house, because she was really visiting Andromeda, the lady in residence. Otherwise, it would be unthinkable to visit a bachelor, even one who was such a close friend, and Rachel never did the unthinkable. Or hardly ever. She had to amend that now, for she often did things that verged on shocking, such as balloon ascents, and those that were completely over the border of shocking into appalling, such as the boxing match.

She stood with her maid on the doorstep of the Strongwycke residence, and was ushered in by the frosty butler. Miss Varens was home. Would Miss Neville wait in the crimson parlor or the drawing room?

Rachel heard voices from the formal parlor down the hallway, the largest receiving room in the house, and wondered why the others were there. She said to Larkson, "I will join my friends. I can tell where they are, thank you." To her maid she said, "Wait in the hallway. I shan't be long."

Ignoring the butler's protestations, she strode down the hall and into the formal parlor. The sight that greeted her was not at all what she expected.

Andromeda, dressed in breeches and a man's shirt, sat cross-legged on a table, watching her brother and Sir Parnell. The two men were squared off, facing each other, and wore black leather mufflers on their hands as they stood, almost in fencing stance. Andromeda turned.

"Rachel, hallo! You are just in time to see a demonstration of the fine art of pugilism."

Staring, not believing her eyes, though Belinda had told her what to expect, Rachel was speechless. Sir Parnell waved one mitted hand, but Colin merely stared. She joined Andromeda, who looked oddly 'right' in her male garb and her casual pose as she never had in frilly dresses and turbans.

"Don't let me stop you," Rachel said, finding her voice.

Colin gave her another long, considering look, and she felt her stomach quiver, but then he turned back to his opponent. The men boxed, clearly pulling their punches, while Andromeda explained the moves and talked about the art and science of pugilism. Rachel could not look away from Colin. He looked magnificent, she thought, in breeches that outlined muscular thighs and a loose shirt open to the middle of his chest and with the sleeves rolled up over muscular forearms. He was not overly hirsute, just that arrow of coarse dark hair down the middle of his chest. Shocking. Simply shocking. Definitely not a sight she should be seeing. That must be the explanation for the palpitations she suffered: she was shocked.

But every move he made strained the seams of his breeches, and he moved smoothly, much better than the older man. Colin was a natural athlete, something Rachel had never realized.

Nor would she have cared in the past, she admitted to herself. Her former view seemed narrow and self-absorbed. Nothing that did not concern her directly had been of interest. How had she lived like that for so many years?

And why now did she see things so differently? Her eyes had been opened and she saw all around her examples of love and tenderness, men and women setting aside their inevitable differences to find bliss in each other's arms.

"Where is Belinda?" Rachel roused herself to ask. Her voice was a little hoarse and she cleared her throat.

"That young friend of Pamela's, Mr. Dexter, asked to take her for a drive and to the Tower to the menagerie. I thought it would make a lovely treat for her—someone closer to her own age, you know. Nice young lad." Andromeda had not taken her eyes off the pair boxing, but her gaze was riveted on her fiancé, not her brother. They had decided they would after all go north with Colin to Corleigh, and Sir Parnell and Andromeda would be married from her home.

Rachel was delighted. She looked forward to their wedding, knowing how much happiness it would bring to the two involved, and how much to Colin, too, to have a brother like Sir Parnell.

"Anything wrong between you two?" Andromeda asked, breaking into her thoughts.

"Between . . ."

"Colin and you."

"Why do you ask that?"

The other woman shrugged and slipped down off the table easily. Her new athleticism seemed to have made her graceful. "Don't know. Just a feeling." She raised her voice and said, "Hey, you two, it is my turn."

"Do you plan to fight me?" Colin said, in a teasing tone, turning from his opponent.

"No, because you will not be as kind to me as Parnell will," she said, laughter in her voice.

Rachel, strangely, felt tears well up in her eyes. She had never heard nor seen Andromeda happier, and it touched her deeply. Of all of them, Andromeda deserved this happiness, this rich reward for being a good sister, a valuable neighbor, and a faithful friend. The saying went that virtue was its own reward, but a tangible recompense was deserved for a lifetime of service to others. No one deserved happiness, long deferred and richly earned, more than Andromeda Varens.

When the mitts were changed from Colin's to Andromeda's hands, she and her lover squared off and began to box, sometimes falling into a laughing clinch. Colin stayed close by them until his sister, with a look and a word, shooed him away. He reluctantly joined Rachel.

Annoyed by his obvious reluctance to speak to her, her first instinct was to snipe at him. She generally made it known when she was angry, but how well had that served as a way to go on? And was she not interpreting his disinclination to join her through her own emotions? It could have nothing to do with her. She would ignore it, for now.

"How odd to see Andromeda so involved in your sport, when she was so against it at first," Rachel said to Colin, determined to begin on a light note. "And yet I do not think I have ever seen her so happy."

"She almost does not seem like my sister," he

replied, his tone bemused. "She said just this morning that the butler disapproves of her, and she doesn't care. Belowstairs opinion used to matter most profoundly to her. Appearances, and all that."

"Maybe it was because she had nothing but appearances to cling to," Rachel said, pensively, finding in those words something to ponder.

He shot her a swift glance, then looked back to the combatants. "I would never have guessed when I went to Sir Parnell for training that he would someday be my brother-in-law." He leaned up against the table and ran one hand through his perspiration-drenched curls.

"It is fortunate that you have so much in common. Your family will be close." Silence fell between them, but Rachel, determined not to ignore what she had really come there to discuss, broke back into awkward speech. "Colin, I wanted to ask you about last night, and . . ."

"Nothing to last night. Just the impulse of the moment, you know."

Rachel fell silent again. It was noteworthy that he knew immediately that she was asking about the kiss, but . . . was that truly all it was to him? It had felt like much more. And yet hadn't she been wondering if men had many different reasons for kissing, only one of which was genuine caring? If that was the question she had come to get an answer to, it appeared that her quest was fulfilled. It had been the impulse of the moment, and nothing more. And yet she could not leave it alone so easily.

The two combatants had stripped off their gloves and approached, arm in arm.

"We are going to cool off in the garden," Andromeda said. "You two are welcome to join us there for lemonade."

Colin was about to follow them, but Rachel caught his arm. "Wait."

When the others were gone, she faced him. "Colin, you say kissing me was the impulse of the moment, but impulses come from somewhere. What did it *mean*?"

"Who knows," he said, irritably. "Why must we poke and prod everything, turn it over and over and assume it means something? Can it not be just be a kiss?"

Hands on her hips, Rachel said to him, "You are just as infuriating now as when you mooned over me relentlessly. Do you know that? Then you were a pathetic puppy, following me around and proposing twice a year. Now you are as closed as a clamshell."

"Maybe there is nothing to examine," he said, his face expressionless.

"How can you say that?" She considered letting it go, stalking out, and going back to not speaking to him. But no. That was letting him off too easy. There had to be something behind his kissing her the previous night, and he owed her an explanation. If he would not talk, then—

She reached up, curled her hand around his neck and pulled him down, kissing him on the lips before he had time to protest.

He didn't protest. His arm snaked around her back, and he pulled her close. She could feel his damp heat through the fine lawn shirt he wore, and the hard, muscled wall of his chest. One kiss became two, and then many. He pressed against her, trapping her against the table at her back, cradling her head in one hand and running his hand down her spine with the other. He consumed her with a ferocious hunger that communicated itself to her in his intensity, his greedy appetite for her. It was thrilling and frightening and bewildering, all at the same time.

Colin, for his part, knew he was lost. Every moment he swore to himself he would stop, and then he would kiss her again, finally separating her velvet lips and tentatively tasting her mouth, dipping into her secret recess even as his body grew hard against her. If she had murmured one protestation he would have stopped, but she was passive in his arms.

Damn. *Damn.* Passive. She was quiescent and unprotesting, not pulling away or demanding he stop, but neither did she match his eagerness. He pulled away from her, wretchedly feeling the throb of lust and passion spiral through him in waves. He stared down into her bewildered eyes, torn between confessing there and then that he still loved her, loved her more than ever, in fact, and walking away. He had been rejected so very many times, and he had no reason to think this time would be any different. He couldn't risk it.

Without a word he strode away, refusing even to look back when she called his name.

Rachel, after a time spent regaining her composure and resettling her bonnet, which was askew, joined Sir Parnell and Andromeda in the garden, where a tiny summerhouse held a table and chairs.

"I must go." Her voice was almost steady; she should be proud of herself. Anyone looking at her would think her as calm as ever, no doubt. Instead all she felt was wretchedly unhappy and unsettled.

Andromeda, her eyes bright with curiosity, walked back through the house with her, but as they approached the front door, she asked, "Did you and Colin talk?"

"I don't think there is anything that we have to talk about anymore. He has changed, and so have I."

"But . . ." The older woman seemed on the verge of saying something, but remained silent.

She bit her lip, and as they came to the door, uncharacteristically pulled Rachel to her in a hug. Her body felt angular, but the embrace was oddly comforting.

"You have changed, Rachel, but it has been a good change."

"Has it?" she asked dully, taking her shawl from her maid. "I used to know what I wanted in my life, and now I am adrift. I do not understand men in the slightest." That was revealing too much. She had not meant to say anything. She smiled at her old friend. "But I am so happy for *you*, Andromeda," Rachel said, squeezing her friend's hands.

"Thank you. I never expected this kind of happiness. I had quite given up. I wish the same for you. Not to give up on it, you know, but to find it."

"Perhaps I am the one who will remain a spinster."

"That would be a shame, especially when you and . . ." She looked over her shoulder, back into the house and shrugged. "You know, the one thing I never expected about marriage was that it would . . . set me free. Love, oddly enough, the closest tie that binds two humans, has a way of doing that . . . setting you free. Free to say and do things you never would have thought possible. I never expected that. I think I thought of marriage as another kind of service, like the church or being a good daughter, but it is so far removed from anything else I have ever experienced."

"I must go," Rachel said, releasing Andromeda's hands.

"Remember that," the older woman said, with a fervency in her tone. "Love can give you great freedom."

"Certainly." Rachel, not at all sure what she meant but anxious to be alone with her thoughts, exited, asking to be remembered to Belinda.

Andromeda, left inside the cold, echoing confines of the great hall, firmed her lips and whirled, striding off to find Colin and give him a piece of her mind.

Twenty

Colin, deeply shaken, sat alone in the library, his head in his hands, staring at the figured carpet. He dug his fingers into his curls and pulled, frustration and confusion ripping at his gut. What was he to think? Rachel had demanded to know what the night before had meant, and then had kissed him. She had definitely made the first move, but his own yearning had overpowered him, and he had let loose all the repressed longing in his soul and body. For a few seconds it had been heaven, until he had realized how quiet she was, passive, quiescent. That was not what he wanted. He wanted her to kiss him back, love him as deeply as he loved and needed her.

He pondered the years of their acquaintance, all the rejections, all the times he had thought he was making progress, only to find she disdained his suit just as always. What was he now to think? With any other girl he would imagine her kiss to mean she liked him and welcomed him as a potential suitor, but he had learned through long hard trial and error—more than anyone else knew, even Andromeda—that it did not do to make assumptions with Rachel. He was as confused as ever.

The library door squeaked open.

"Colin? What are you doing sitting in the gloom like this?"

"Go away, Andy. I have things to think about."

"Hmm. 'Things' meaning Rachel Neville?"

"Not your business, old girl. Leave it alone." His tone was grim, he knew, and he meant it to be. This was no time for anyone to be bothering him. He wanted to be alone with his misery.

"I won't."

That figured. Andromeda was more stubborn than any other woman he knew.

"Colin, I don't know what went on between you two just now," she said, coming over and crouching at his knee. "But I do know that when she left she looked . . . confused. Troubled."

He laughed shortly. "Poor, poor Rachel! She is certainly troubled. Probably because I won't propose again so she can reject me one more time."

"Colin! Don't sound so bitter!"

"Don't tell me how to sound."

"But she's not like that anymore."

"You are such an innocent, Andy." He stared into her dark eyes and shook his head. "Just because you are the soul of honesty does not mean most women are like you. Women *are* like that. *Rachel* is like that. She has led me down the garden path before and I fear she is doing it again, just to amuse herself now that all her suitors have . . . well, no, that is not true." He thrust his fingers through his tousled hair again and clutched at it in frustration. "She could have her pick of men to court her if she wanted. God knows there are dozens of them fools for her. Just like me."

"Not just like you! You know her; they don't.

Colin, give her a chance. Believe that people can change. It is possible."

"I have thought so before . . ."

"I told you then that you were a fool!" she said, vigorously. "I knew what she was about, but you didn't listen to me. She was an unhappy, bitter girl then. I see such a difference in her now, and you are a great dolt if, feeling the way you do . . ."

"You have no idea how I feel," he said, exasperated. Andromeda had always tried to order his life, but it was enough. He was a man and would not stand for it anymore. "Just go away, Andy."

"Do you love her?"

"Shut up and go away!"

He was being unconscionably rude, and he regretted it immediately. He stood and stretched, his sister rising as he did. He took her shoulders, gazed directly into her eyes and said, "I will manage my own life. I will not die without Miss Rachel Neville, I promise you that."

Andromeda's eyes filled with tears and she laid her palm flat on his cheek. "I just want you to be as happy as I am, little brother. And if you love Rachel as I love Parnell, then only having her will make you happy. Life with love is so . . . so full and rich, as if all the colors are new and all the sights you have ever seen are fresh. It changes you, I think. Transforms you."

"Oh, Andy! What will I do with you now that you have turned so wise?" He gave her a quick, uncharacteristic hug and as swiftly released her. "Once we had unrequited love in common; you with Haven and me with Rachel. Now I am alone. I don't think I like it."

"Then you do still love her."

He sighed, unwilling or unable to battle it any more. "I do. I love her more than ever, with every fiber of my being."

She frowned at him, her expression full of puzzlement. "How can you love her if you think so poorly of her, that she would lead you on purposely yet again? I never did understand that."

He frowned, wondering about that himself. How could you love someone you didn't trust? Was it merely lust, then, or frustrated desire? No, there was more, much more, in the tangled web of his feelings for Miss Rachel Neville. It was deeper, more complex, a part of his soul and his definition of himself, and had been for years. And yet it was not just a habit he had gotten into, as he had begun to believe. "I have always known that there is something within her, something fine and precious buried under the layers of social manners and elegant affectation. I love that. I want that. But I am resigned now that it is so deeply buried she might never let it come forth."

"Or maybe you are blinded by years of rejection," Andromeda said gently, reaching out and tousling his curls just as if he were a boy still. They were silent for a few moments in the vast faintly musty cavern that was the Strongwycke library. When Andromeda spoke again, her voice was hushed, quiet, and yet rich with feeling. "Have you ever considered that perhaps you have been underestimating her and her ability to change, to grow? Maybe she is now all that you thought she could be."

"Why?" He shrugged and shook his head. "No, Andy, I am no different than in the past. I have no more money, no better status, nor am I better looking. I am still just me. Homely, uncouth Colin. How can I believe her feelings toward me would have changed?"

"Because the change never needed to come from you, it needed to be within her. And she *is* different, more thoughtful, more . . ."

Finished with the subject and sick of speculation, Colin turned his sister and gave her a push toward the door. He was tired of all of this introspection. It gained him nothing that he could see or feel or touch, and that was all that mattered in the end. Here and now was all he had, all he would ever have. "Go back to your knight in shining armor and leave me to sort out my romantic woes on my own. I promise I will be as happy as a grig at your wedding and shall dance 'til dawn."

Alone in the Haven House drawing room—everyone's least favorite room, and therefore private most of the time—Rachel, curled up on the grim, indescribably ugly sofa, and sat staring out the muddy glass to the street scene trying to understand her own feelings, much less Colin's continued rejection of her in contrast to his enthusiastic participation in their kisses.

He had enjoyed it as much as she had. And she had liked it, not in any remote sense, but because it was Colin. She had wanted to kiss him. *Him.* Colin Varens, old friend and neighbor, companion of her youth. The previous night had awakened some hunger that was not yet sated. Maybe it never would be. His ravenous kisses of that morning had just sharpened her appetite into a craving. She hadn't known how to understand it, hadn't imagined the force with which it would consume her, and so had gone still, quiet, trying to fathom her reactions to Colin's caresses. But the hunger had not abated, and maybe never would.

There was a dreadful notion. *Imagine,* she thought, *going around all the time hungry for what I can never have, knowing in my heart that no matter how much I need the other person—*

The thought arrested her and she stared blankly out the window. That was exactly what Colin must have felt for the last five or six years, ever since the first time he proposed—after considerable encouragement from her—only to be told no, she would never marry him. Time after time he had proposed, sometimes obliquely, sometimes with an outright declaration, professing his love and devotion, swearing undying fidelity. And she had always rejected him.

And yet she had taken for granted that Colin loved her and would always love her.

Had that love that he had professed to be eternal finally died? Had seeing her in London's milieu, set against the backdrop of hundreds of lovely ladies, many of them eager for his attentions, finally cooled his ardor? It was a logical assumption to make.

But not if she was to judge by his kisses.

She touched her lips. At seventeen she had let him kiss her once, a very chaste kiss, and only fleeting. She had felt nothing and had never let him repeat the experiment, sure she would feel no more than that one time. In truth, she had been happy she did not feel the tingling a girl once described to her. It had sounded horribly . . . earthy.

It was safer to be cool, and she had always been happy that she seemed to be cold by nature. Frozen, one did not feel pain if someone left—or died. Too much of life was lived on an emotional plane, she had always thought. Poets raved on and on about the all-consuming fires of love, the desperation of unrequited passion. They maundered on about bitter jealousy and rage, despair. She was seldom troubled by feelings of anger or jealousy, fear or sadness. She had liked it that way, been happy in her coolness.

So what was wrong with her now? Why were her emotions in a tumult, her thinking muddled and confused?

She traced a heart on the dusty pane of glass. The servants were clearly not doing their job in this part of the house, she thought, wiping her finger on the brocade of the hideous sofa. Her mother was failing in her usual strict discipline, but then she had been distracted lately, with Grand ill.

She should be doing something, Rachel thought. She should go out shopping or to the bookstore or she should go visiting. She owed many visits before she left London, and just did not have the energy, it seemed, for any of them. She frankly did not care.

What was wrong with her?

Feelings, so long restrained or submerged, raced through her constantly, leaving her wretched with a longing for peace. But no matter how hard she tried, she could not find the way back to her former poise, and, strangely, was not even sure that she wanted to. For this emotional life, she was discovering, had compensations. Apart from her tumultuous longings, she had found that there were pleasant moments in her newly emotional life.

Belinda had insisted on walking arm in arm with her just the other day, and it had warmed her. Giddily, they had sung a silly song as they walked in the park, and she had not cared when people stared. And Andromeda! They had long had a difficult and cool relationship, and Rachel knew it was because of her rejection of Colin's suit. Rachel feared it also had derived from her own disdain for Andromeda, whom she had considered just an odd spinster, negligible at best, strange at worst. But the woman had been so very kind to her lately, and she had found in her almost an older sister. Life had its difficult moments, but also its rewards.

And most of all, there was Colin. She must face facts. She very much feared that after all this time, and all her continued rejection, she had fallen in love with him.

Kissing him had thawed the last frozen bits of her heart, and it had stung, like frostbitten fingers warming near a fire. There was the tingle and the sting. She thought she could enjoy kissing him often, if he would respond as eagerly as he had that morning. Surely that must mean something, his fervent response, or was it different for men? Could they kiss someone and yet not truly care about them?

She was no idiot. She had heard the whispered tales of girls led astray by a man with promises and then abandoned. And she knew men kept women for their own bodily pleasure with no attachment.

She knew what the marriage bed meant, both to men and to women. It was described by her mother as a sordid duty, but she had known her mother exaggerated its unpleasantness to women, for surely there would not be so many children born in the world if patriotism, a desire to repopulate their isolated island after the ravages of war, was the only reason. Most women she knew were not that patriotic.

But what she had never considered was, what if it was—scandalous thought—enjoyable, the earthy side of begetting children? If kissing was a part of it, and she supposed it must be, for she would certainly demand it be, then it could prove to be . . . entertaining. She laid her flaming cheek on the back of the sofa, wondering at the turn of her thoughts, and traced heart shapes on the brocade back. What a moonling she had become!

Colin. If she should marry him, would he come naked to bed, and would they . . . she buried her face in her arm. Perhaps, after all, this love she thought she now felt for Colin was merely physical, some strange awakening of her womanly self.

Again she traced the brocade design. No, she did not think that theory would hold up to the light of reason. If that was true, if what she felt for him was no more than the physical longing a woman might feel for an attractive man, she would not have been so worried for him in the ring. Seeing him hit had left her distraught, horribly fearful for his safety. And acknowledging those feelings had disturbed her more than she would ever admit to anyone.

The familiar tap-tap-tap of a cane sounded in the hall, and the door opened. Rachel looked up as her grandmother came into the room. She looked so tired and frail. Sometimes it seemed as if willpower alone kept her going. There was another difficult relationship she was experiencing anew. She and her grandmother had never been close, and yet, seeing her ill, she had realized how much she treasured the troublesome old woman. It had occurred to her that their differences over the years had partly been due to her feeling that her grandmother had never been misled by Rachel's careful, ladylike demeanor.

"I thought I would find you here," the old woman said. "Hiding out from your mother?"

"Not really," Rachel said, hopping up from the sofa and moving to pull out a chair for her grandmother. "Here, Grand, sit. You should not be up so much. And whatever happened to that Bath chair Mother purchased for you?"

"I sent it to Yorkshire." She dropped into the chair with a groan. "Once I am there, your mother and I are going to move into the dower house, we think, and have a joyful time redecorating it. We have ordered new furnishings, wallcoverings, paint, marble tiles . . . all manner of hideously expensive rubbish. She is still angry with Haven and thinks to punish him by moving out of Haven Court to Haven Wood." The old woman's eyes twinkled. "I shall tell him that if he wants his peace he should act heartbroken and demand she move back to the big house! It will keep her with me for years!"

"How will you two live together? You can barely stand to be in the same room without bickering."

The twinkle softened and a smile loosened the pursestring wrinkles around the old woman's mouth. "Lydia, for all her bluster and misguided notions, is a good woman. I fear I have been horribly hard on her for too many years. I would like the opportunity to make up for that now. As short as the time left to me is, I would make good use of it."

Rachel shook her head and curled back up on the brocade sofa. "Everything feels like it is changing. Where shall I live?"

"Where do you want to live?"

"With Colin." It was immediate, the response so quick it must have been from her heart. She hid her flaming face in her arms for a moment, but then looked up to meet the dowager's eyes.

Grand did not seem surprised. "And what is stopping you? The puppy has always been mad for you."

"Not now. I think I have killed all those tender feelings. I have been so cruel. He will never ask me to marry him now. I have rejected him too many times."

The old lady leaned forward on her cane. "Tell him to come see me. I will set him straight. I have done it before to the country turnip!"

Rachel thought back to just a short time before, when Colin, finally accepting her last rejection of his suit, had turned around just days later and asked her younger sister to marry him. Pamela had already received Strongwycke's proposal, and Colin's had confused her terribly, because she had always fancied herself in love with him. Rachel raised the specter of that ill-timed proposal to her grandmother. "What did that mean? How could he want to marry me one day, and then ask Pammy to marry him two days later?"

The woman snorted. "He never truly wanted to marry her! Just thought she would make a com-

fortable wife and a friend for his sister. The lad
has poor control over his impulses. That makes
him a good fighter, I suppose."

Impulses. Like the impulse to kiss her, she supposed. And yet, watching him box with Sir
Parnell, she had to think that boxing, contrary to
her grandmother's opinion, required a great
deal of control over one's impulses. One could
not just lash out, but must choose the best time
and strike wisely.

But nonetheless, it was a relief, hearing her
opinion that the proposal to her little sister had
just been an impulsive gesture. Colin's proposal
to Pamela had hurt and puzzled her. She hadn't
quite known why then. Now she understood herself a fraction better. She had been jealous and
put out, in truth. "Grandmother, what can I do?
How can I make him see that I have changed,
that I . . . I love him." There, it was said, for better or worse, and it did not feel so bad, admitting
that she loved him and yet he might not love her.

Oh. That *did* feel bad.

"You will have to be bold, I am afraid. Men do
not like to look foolish, and I am afraid you publicly rejected him once too often. Not that you did
the wrong thing, my dear. No woman should say
yes when her heart says no. And yet for the longest
time I believed that a marriage could be perfectly
good without love. Mine was for many years." She
gazed toward the hearth, her blue eyes becoming
misty with remembrance. "Then, oddly, I fell in
love with my husband after I lost my second child.
He was heartbroken, and I thought it was because
it was another son, and then I found out his pain
was for me, for what I had gone through. My mar-

riage was never the same. Love changed everything. I found out that marriage with love is so much better than without."

Rachel gazed at her grandmother, trying to see the young woman within her, trying to trace the image held only in the portrait in their gallery now of a lovely woman with blazing blue eyes, wearing panniered skirts, her hair dressed high and powdered. It was too hard. Grand had always been an old woman to her.

"Why did it change everything?" she asked.

The elderly woman swiveled her watery gaze to her middle grandchild. "It blessed my heart."

Blessed my heart. What a lovely phrase. Rachel sighed. "What should I do?"

"If you love your baby baronet, and think he loves you in return, then you will have to find a way, some bold gesture, that will let him see you will not treat him shabbily again. My dear, do whatever it takes if he is the one you would marry."

Twenty-one

Colin, in a new suit he did not like and had been scandalized at the cost of—if he had not intended to make it do for Andromeda's wedding, he would not have purchased it—strolled around the perimeter of the Codstead ballroom, a crowded, stuffy room with too many potted palms for its limited size. He had the impression the baroness, Lady Codstead, knowing how few people were still in London and wanting her ball to seem a squeeze, had replaced humans with palms and ferns. It felt like a tropical forest.

But Andromeda had insisted they all come, for this was the last night before they planned to start their journey north, home. Home. Corleigh's green hills and rocky fells beckoned. He should never have been gone this long, more than two months. It was unconscionable when there was so much work to be done. He had a farm manager who was perfectly capable of looking after everything, but he could not bear to be draining Corleigh's precious resources by spending time in London. They could not have stayed this long if it hadn't been for Lord Strongwycke's kind loan of his home. That would be their first duty, to return Belinda to her home at Shadow

Manor, Strongwycke's northern estate in the Lakes District.

It would be good to see little Pammy, all grown up and married and mistress of a large household. How the last two months had changed all of their lives!

He stopped and watched the dancers. Parnell and Andromeda were waltzing, their two gaunt, tall figures standing out in the smattering of shorter, punier specimens as they glided across the floor, surprisingly graceful. Though he should not be surprised. To watch them box was to watch a light-footed dance of a sort. The knight and the spinster sparred often, their athletic grace a salutary lesson to anyone who thought that boxing was just a fight.

Their sessions just as often ended with an embarrassing bout of kisses and whispered exchanges, not the usual end to a boxing match. He had never seen his sister so happy.

He had to be content they had spent time in London, for Andromeda had found her match, a man who would appreciate her for exactly who she was, a strong-minded, independent, and sometimes eccentric woman. He had always thought he would marry and his sister would remain single, but it appeared he was the one meant to be alone. He could not see himself marrying while he still loved Rachel, and he couldn't imagine not loving Rachel. It was a bind, to be sure. He turned his mind away from his romantic problem.

The one thing he would miss about London would be his boxing. He had enjoyed not only the athletic aspect to his sport, but also the notoriety it brought him. He had gained acceptance and a measure of fame, and found that he liked it. He even had an idea to start a boxing club among Lesleydale lads, and that would keep him—and them—busy throughout the long and sometimes tedious Yorkshire winter.

This ball was a dull one, he finally decided. He had done his duty and danced with the daughters of the house. They were pleasant young ladies, but he did not like the way the eldest was eyeing him and trying to maneuver him into a walk in the minuscule conservatory. He had feinted and parried and ducked away when she was otherwise engaged. Now he was thinking that a last modest spot of gambling at cards would finish off his London stay, though he was no gambler and would never lose more than a guinea or two before becoming bored. Turning to head to the card room, he glimpsed Rachel coming in alone, breathtakingly beautiful in a simple white gown, a wreath of white roses around her coronet of braids. He took in a deep shaky breath and let it out, slowly.

God, but he loved her. And he always would.

She had spoken of going to visit Pamela for a while once they were back up north, and he had to be glad, for as friendly as their two families were, he would have to see her often and it hurt him in some deep unexplored region under his ribcage every time he saw her and realized all over again that she would never be his wife. It was not just her beauty, though that was stunning, that he regretted. No, it was so much more than that.

He saw her as a rose, blooming now, almost full-blown. But even when the bloom had withered, desiccating like one of the roses in Andromeda's dry arrangements, he would love her and think her beautiful. They would get old, perhaps both single, and still see each other often, remembering the kisses they had shared one enchanted London Season. And he would still love her. But he would never plague her with his suit again. Rejection at this stage would wound too deeply.

She saw him and moved toward him, gliding gracefully, as if she floated across the ballroom floor. One more dance with her would not hurt, surely. It would be something to remember in that barren future he envisioned. Though he amended it now, looking at her. She would not be single for long. Andromeda had been right about one thing: Rachel had changed, at least in her behavior, though he did not believe her heart had changed. He had always seen a fine, sensitive core beneath the surface hardness. She was more open now, more glowing, and even more beautiful as a result.

Any man alive would want that angel of perfection . . . but no, she was not perfect. She was flawed, but flawed in the same way the most exquisite of world masterpieces were, faulty and vibrant and ineffably beautiful clear down to her heart. And all the more incredible for the flaws.

He found that he was walking toward her, eagerly, his step quickening. Her lovely eyes were wide, her expression anxious.

"You did come," she said as she approached. "I had hoped you would."

He was taken aback by her enthusiastic greeting. "I did. We leave the day after tomorrow, so this will be our last social outing."

She joined her hands with his in the middle of the ballroom floor. He wished they weren't wearing gloves. Damned social nuisances, anyway! He would give anything to feel her flesh, warm, silky, cradled in his rough hands. He halted his wayward thoughts and gave her a tentative smile.

Another piece started, and couples swirled around them. "We leave next week," Rachel said. "Haven and Jane arrive tomorrow. You will be able to see them before you go. They have something they want you to take to Pamela and Strongwycke for them, a gift."

Silence. He held her hand still, looking down at the fine silk of her glove, the dainty hand in his. "Will you dance with me?" he asked. "One more time before I leave?"

She smiled, a brilliant, ethereal smile. "One more time before everything changes," she said.

He took her in his arms. How could he ever bear to let her go?

Rachel felt Colin's awkwardness as he stumbled through the steps of what had turned out to be one of the newer dances. It didn't matter. He was a country gentleman, he eschewed poetry—except the few snippets he had memorized to try to impress her when she was younger—and he preferred a plain dish over French cooking. She loved London and poetry and elegance. She liked parties and balls and pretty gowns. And none of it mattered.

She knew his heart. And yet what she was about to do was take a calculated risk. She would look ridiculous, and appearances had always mattered to her so much. As they danced, she glanced around the ballroom. Some of the *ton's* fiercest gossips were there, and before too long her outré behavior would be the talk of many a visit the next day. Lady Codstead would be grateful, at least. Anything that made one's ball the talk of Society could only be a good thing.

She gazed up at Colin. How had she come to know her own heart? Had it really started with an unfamiliar jolt of physical attraction? It had made her think about Colin more closely, certainly, to find that his presence made her tremble. She had had to explore why such a weird phenomenon was occurring to her.

As the music died, she reached up one gloved hand and touched his cheek, tracing the hard line of his strong jaw. He gazed down at her, his dark brows drawn down, puzzlement in his eyes. Andromeda and Parnell, both aware of what was about to happen, were close by.

"Colin," Rachel said in a loud, unnatural tone. "I have something to say to you, and I wish to say it in front of everyone here."

Lady Codstead, near the band, shushed them, her green eyes avid and staring. Always on the fringes of the *ton*, always wanting more, the woman could, perhaps, sense her social fortune changing. One outrageous occurrence at her ball and she would be the talk of the *ton*. Her reputation would be made.

"What do you have to say? Do you not want to be more private?" Colin said, glancing around at the staring eyes.

"No. What I have to say I want to say here and now."

One unfortunate musician drew his bow across his violin, and above that Lady Codstead could be heard shrieking. "Not now, you dolt. Listen!"

Rachel bit her lip to keep from giggling. She took a deep breath and put her hands on Colin's shoulders. "Colin, I have been haughty and unpleasant to you for many years now."

"Rachel, I . . ."

She put one finger over his mouth. "Shush. It will be your turn to speak in a moment." She swallowed hard. This was more difficult than she had expected, but she shut out the crowd and stared into Colin's honest brown eyes. "I have been haughty and unpleasant. I have made grave errors in judgment. And I have, on occasion, been cruel to you. I regret that most of all, for you never did anything to deserve that. You have always been kind to me. You have a strong and honest heart."

He was silent, now, waiting.

"I will make no excuses, except to say that Society led me to believe that social standing was all important, and I was silly enough to believe it for a time. But a marquess is not better than a baronet. It is the man, not the title, and you are twice the man Yarnell ever was. I was a fool not to see that."

This next part was the hardest.

"I love you."

A collective gasp greeted her plain announcement, and a buzz of gossiping whispers broke out, halted only as she continued.

"I love you, and if you were to ask me now to marry you, I would say yes."

He was trembling, but whether it was mirth,

anger, or emotion, she could not tell from his impassive face. She searched his eyes, but could read nothing, no laughter, no censure, no joy or anger.

Colin felt no desire to laugh, nor was he angry. He was stunned, yes, but thrilled to his core. And it was not just her lovely words, but the honesty he could see in her clear eyes and the lack of all artifice. She had dropped her social manners, and now before him stood the woman he had always known lay in her heart, the sweet, vulnerable core of Rachel. And she was afraid. He could see the fear, the fear of rejection, the fear of being too late. He could make her wait, could taunt her, but why? He need only tell the truth.

"I love you," he whispered, hoarse and shaking. Tears rose in her eyes, though she could only have barely heard his words over the swelling murmur. He became aware of the probing eyes, the curious glances, the giggles and stares and curiosity.

"Come away from here," he said, taking her arm and leading her to the open doors on one side of the room.

The terrace was the size of a billiard table and it was crowded with even more potted palms and topiary trees in tortured shapes. But two people in love, wound together into a tight clutch, did not take up much room. There was certainly enough room for a man and woman to hold each other and whisper words of love.

Epilogue

Autumn folded its arms around Corleigh, the mellow stone melting into the gold and bronze shades of burr oak and birch and alder. Inside, the bite of the autumn winds was cut by banked fires warming the public rooms and by frequent lovemaking between the new mistress of the house, Lady Varens, and her besotted husband, Sir Colin. The summer wedding, a joint affair with Rachel and Colin and Andromeda and Sir Parnell joining their lives together in one ceremony for both, had been the talk of the county. Even now, months later, folks would nod wisely and say they had never seen so much love on one woman's face as on the lovely visage of the new Lady Varens. *'Tis almost indecent,* some said, *how much she worships her homely husband, and she so beautiful!*

Colin didn't give a damn what people said. He was a happy man.

He sat in his cramped library and answered a letter from his sister, some of which dealt with practicalities. She was asking that a few of her favorite pieces of furniture, left to her specifically by their parents, be shipped down to her new home. But much of her writing was crossed lines over crossed lines of happy babble.

Rachel tapped on the door and entered, crossing the floor and standing before her husband. "Colin," she said, softly. "Can we talk?"

He moved away from the desk and opened his arms, and she sat on his lap, squirming around enough to make herself comfortable and her husband uncomfortable. He relaxed into the now familiar budding warmth in his body at her proximity, desire for her flooding him with heat. But she clearly had something on her mind, and he would listen before he tried to tempt her into going upstairs to their chamber with him. If he ever got enough of her, he would be surprised.

"What should we talk about?" he asked, and was surprised to see her blush.

"I am so horribly ignorant in some ways," she said, glancing away and fixing her gaze on the grate in the fireplace.

"Ignorant?"

"About . . . about men. Their physical needs."

He chuckled and pulled her to him, kissing her gently and cradling her against his chest. Lovemaking had been somewhat of a shock to her, and the first few times he was afraid she did not enjoy it overmuch. But he had worked hard to bring her to ecstasy, and after the first time she had experienced sexual enjoyment, a surprised *oh* of pleasure his first hint, he had seen a difference in her eyes. He found the more he kissed her, the more enthusiastically she participated, and since kissing Rachel was always a joy, they quickly found a pleasing rhythm for them both.

"That is one thing I can probably help you

with," he said, moving to make himself more comfortable and feeling her bottom settle on him provocatively.

Her color deepened as her breathing quickened. "I need to know something."

"Yes," he murmured, kissing her neck and letting his hand move to cradle her breast.

"Colin, I'm serious!"

"So am I." He moved, settling his arousal more comfortably and pulling her soft day dress up over her knees. But then he could feel that she had gone still and he met her gaze.

Her bottom lip trembled. Rachel did not cry easily. Something had to be wrong. He felt a jolt of fear.

"Rach, what is it? Is everything all right?"

"Yes. It truly is. But I need to know something. Sarah said something to me, and I need to know if it is true."

"Sarah?"

"My lady's maid. You know, the one who stutters."

"Yes, I remember now." He kissed her gently, and said, "She said something. Ask away. What is troubling you?"

"She said that if men are . . . are deprived of their wives' attention for any reason . . ." She stopped and stared again. "Say I was to go away for a few months."

"Are you going somewhere? May I come?"

"Colin, listen! She said . . . she said that if a man was deprived of his wife's . . . . attention, that he would go to someone else."

"What on earth are you talking about?"

Rachel sighed. "She said that men can't help it.

If their wife is . . . . away, then men turn to a maid or a bar serving girl for . . . relief."

"Good God," he said, almost shouted. "I can't speak for other men, Rachel, but no woman in the world could ever replace you. Why would any man go seeking when he has the most lovely, most desirable . . ."

"But that's just it, Colin. What if I was . . . oh, *away* for a while?"

"Here," he said, panic beginning to clutch his heart. "Are you going somewhere? To visit Pammy? I could go with you. Or at least take you there and come and fetch you back."

"No, Colin, I am not going anywhere. Not for quite a while, I think. But . . ." She broke off in confusion and hid her face in his shoulder.

His mind whirled. She loved him, he knew it, but at first she had not enjoyed lovemaking too much. Perhaps she wanted a break from it. Had he been too demanding, thinking only of his own greedy need and not her delicacy?

"Rachel, you can tell me anything. If I have been too demanding of you, or if you wish me to not . . . not visit your room so often," he said, trying to be delicate, "I will do anything you want, even leave you alone."

"Idiot," she said, hitting his shoulder with his fist. "No, but in a very few months I might not feel up to some of our more . . . vigorous games."

Was she feeling ill? She must have seen the bewilderment on his face.

"Colin, I am sure now, so I may as well tell you. In the spring, we are going to be . . . three."

"Be three? What on earth?" Something occurred

to him, and he swiftly looked at her face for confirmation. "Rachel, we're going to have a baby?"

She nodded, her eyes bright. "Yes. Sometime in late May, we think."

They held each other for a long half hour then, murmuring words of love and happiness, their joy overflowing. And yet they were both realists. Sometimes babies were not born, or born dead, and sometimes there was danger to the mother. There was a touch of trepidation in their joy, but it could only sweeten it, not dim it. Love would see them through whatever happened, happy or sad.

Finally, he gazed down into her face and said, "Why did Sarah fill your head with such nonsense, that men took out their lust on some other girl when their wife was with child?"

"Sarah said that she heard it from one of the girls at the Tippling Swan. She said that men couldn't help themselves and that when their wife was away or sick or with child, men naturally found another woman to fulfill their needs."

Gently, he cradled her in his arms and said, "Rachel, it is true. It is true of some men. But you, you lucky girl, chose me, and since I was about twenty I have wanted no woman like I want and need you."

"Does that mean you have never been with another woman since then?"

He swallowed hard. "Uh, not exactly."

"What do you mean?"

"Like any young fellow I . . . well, I sowed my wild oats, as the saying goes. Even though I loved you all along, I did make love with the occasional . . ."

He saw her bottom lip protrude and knew she was swiftly becoming angry. How to explain?

There was no explanation. But he had to do the best he could. "Rachel, every young man feels compelled to find physical union with women. But one day I came to understand that I was . . . well, soiling my thoughts of you by taking other women to bed. And I stopped."

"When was that, in London?"

"Don't be petulant, Rach. No, it was . . . do you remember your twentieth birthday party?"

"I do. That was four years ago."

Colin stared at the fire. "I found you crying in the library at Haven Court."

She nodded and buried her face in his collar. "I was missing Father," she said, sniffling. "I still do. Oh, Colin, he would be so happy to know . . . to know we are together. He loved you like a son."

"I know. And he knows about us, I am sure of it. If . . . if we have a son I would like to name him for your father."

"Really?" She looked up into his eyes. "Oh, Colin, thank you. You are the best of husbands. But I interrupted you."

"You were crying, and I held you for an hour. From that moment on, I knew I could not be with another woman. I only ever wanted you. That was four years ago."

"I have never doubted you," she said, simply. "It is just that this, the physical side of loving you so much, is all new to me. I assumed, when Yarnell and I were engaged, that he would have a mistress, and it did not disturb me in the slightest. But if you ever went to another woman, and I knew you were doing to her what we do . . ." She left the rest unsaid.

"I never could," he said, simply.

"I love you," she said.

He touched her flat belly, marveling that they had created something so wonderful. "In the spring?" he said.

"In the late spring. May. Or early June."

He was silent again. It was almost too much happiness, especially when he considered that six months ago he had rushed to London, fearing the worst, only to find out that Rachel was engaged. And now she was his wife. His lover. His life.

She slid off his lap and he stood, wrapping her in his arms as the afternoon light played across the painted walls.

"I can't believe how much has happened in just six months," she said, echoing his thoughts. Haven and Jane married and almost ready to have their first child, and Pammy and Strong-wycke and Andromeda and Parnell all married. All of life different. And even Grand and Mother, living together at the dower house. Our lives have all changed."

"And new life beginning."

"And new life beginning," she whispered. "You won't box anymore, Colin, will you?"

He put his arm around her and led her toward the door, to take her upstairs. "Rach, please don't start that again. I have to have some outlet . . ."

"But you have exercise," she said wickedly, tweaking his square chin. "And I do not want the father of my child . . ."

"*Our* child. And if it is a boy, you know I will teach him boxing, just as I do the village lads."

"Colin, you will not! Or if you do, you will teach our girls, too! But no, I forbid you . . ."

Their bickering continued as they walked slowly up the stairs, but once inside her bedroom, it stopped. There was no time, and their mouths were more pleasantly engaged.

ABOUT THE AUTHOR

Donna Simpson lives with her family in Canada. She is currently working on her next Zebra Regency romance, to be published in 2004. Donna loves to hear from readers, and you may write to her c/o Zebra Books. Please include a self-addressed stamped envelope if you wish a reply.

Put a Little Romance in Your Life With
Constance O'Day-Flannery

__Bewitched
0-8217-6126-9

$5.99US/$7.50CAN

__The Gift
0-8217-5916-7

$5.99US/$7.50CAN

__Once in a Lifetime
0-8217-5918-3

$5.99US/$7.50CAN

__Time-Kept Promises
0-8217-5963-9

$5.99US/$7.50CAN

__Second Chances
0-8217-5917-5

$5.99US/$7.50CAN

Call toll free **1-888-345-BOOK** to order by phone, use this coupon to order by mail, or order online at **www.kensingtonbooks.com**.

Name_____

Address _____

City_____ State _____ Zip _____

Please send me the books I have checked above.

I am enclosing	$_____
Plus postage and handling*	$_____
Sales tax (in New York and Tennessee only)	$_____
Total amount enclosed	$_____

*Add $2.50 for the first book and $.50 for each additional book.

Send check or money order (no cash or CODs) to:

Kensington Publishing Corp., Dept. C.O., 850 Third Avenue, New York, NY 10022

Prices and numbers subject to change without notice.

All orders subject to availability.

Visit our website at **www.kensingtonbooks.com**.

More Zebra Regency Romances